The
BANK
of the
RIVER

The

BANK

of the

RIVER

MICHAEL RICHAN

DANTULL

By the author

The Bank of the River
A Haunting in Oregon

THE BANK OF THE RIVER

ISBN-10: 1-49042-520-9 / ISBN-13: 978-1-49042-520-7

First printing: June 2013

www.michaelrichan.com

For Max and Thomas

One

Steven Hall slowed down his Accord as he approached the trailer court. It was dark and rainy and a little difficult to make out directions. He noticed reflective numbers on stakes near the ground by each trailer. Seven, eight...he was headed to 56, the trailer of John and Debra Peterson. He turned a tight corner, and no less than four signs encouraged him to slow down ("Children play here!"). He tapped the brakes and let the car slowly idle forward over the first of many speed bumps.

The time on the car's display read 7:20. He was too early. He didn't want to get there before 7:30, the time Debra had said she would meet him. Seven-thirty was after John left for work, an evening shift. Originally Steven had wanted to talk to John. Earlier that day Steven had called him, asking if he would meet with him to discuss John's father. John had hung up on him, but Debra had called him back later to say she would talk with him – but only after John had left for work.

Surely it wouldn't take ten minutes to drive through this trailer court, but as the car inched along past empty lot 15 he was beginning to wonder. Up ahead he had to turn either left or right, but he couldn't make out which direction the numbers ran. He chose right and drifted until the next reflective number appeared. If he had to backtrack, no problem – better to be a little late in this case than too early.

John's father used to own the house where Steven now lived. Fifteen years earlier, he committed suicide in the house; since that time, the house had gone through a succession of owners, ending with Steven. Steven bought the house two months ago. He was fully aware of its history (no thanks to the agent) and fully discounted the idea that it was, as a previous owner had described it, unlivable.

Just after he moved in, Steven received notice from his company that their office was shutting down and relocating overseas. Steven was too highly paid to be offered a transfer – overseas, all costs would be cut, especially labor. So he found himself in a new house with a moderate severance, time on his hands, and a desire to relax and enjoy a sabbatical before entering the next phase of his life.

But the relaxation never happened. The first few weeks he was in the house, he wrote off most of the occurrences (he hated that word, it made things sound supernatural, but he didn't know what else to call them) as normal adjustments to a new house. Every house makes noises. This house, built in the 1950s, creaked and popped throughout the day as the temperature changed. Plumbing could make banging noises for a variety of reasons. There were sounds from the neighborhood that he wasn't accustomed to yet. None of this was unusual, and Steven adjusted to the idiosyncrasies of the place. But recently there had been some occurrences (ugh) that he hadn't been able to adjust to.

The worst was last night, and it had spurred him to make phone calls this morning to try and find out if there was more about the house than he knew from the research he had conducted before he bought it.

From the first night he'd lived there, Steven had endured the sound of someone knocking in the middle of the night. When it happened, it was loud enough to wake him up, and for a moment he'd think he must have dreamt it. But then it would come again: four distant raps, muffled, as though coming from the front door of the house. The first time it happened he went to the door, expecting someone to be there. When he found no one, he inspected the house thoroughly and went back to bed. When it happened the next night, he began to suspect neighbor kids, so he set up a webcam and let it run for several days. It showed nothing. The knocking continued every night. It always woke him up, even if he tried to sleep through it. Four knocks, twice in a row, separated by about ten seconds.

A week ago he had the old galvanized pipes in the house replaced with new plastic ones. The plumber assured him this would resolve the problem. Galvanized pipes slowly corrode inside, and his were sixty years old, constricting the water flow and likely creating a banging sound now and again. Eight thousand dollars and four days later he went to bed hoping he'd solved the problem, but at three a.m. the knocking came again. Steven had, for weeks, convinced himself that whatever was causing the knockings was something structural about the house, and that if he could find the problem and fix it, it would stop. But now he was running out of options. And, being honest with himself, the knocking had never really sounded like pipes. It wasn't a banging sound, it was a knocking. It sounded like a human hand knocking on a door when someone is announcing their presence or wants to be let in.

He passed trailer 32. *Maybe I should just rent a trailer and leave the house*, he thought. A rent payment in addition to a mortgage payment doesn't make sense when you're unemployed. Steven's house had quickly gone underwater after he closed, so he knew if he tried to list it he wouldn't get what he owed. And it would be a hard sell. Its history was the reason he'd been able to buy it so cheaply in the first place. For some reason, people don't like living in houses that have experienced death, or worse, suicide. This seemed completely irrational to Steven at the time he bought the place. Now he was beginning to wonder.

Steven was always rational, circumspect, skeptical. It was the thing that had, at first, attracted but eventually repelled his wife. They divorced seven years ago in what had seemed to Steven a completely ridiculous way; suddenly, with a barrage of complaints from left field that left him bewildered, and no willingness to explore solutions. Jason, his son, was now in college learning to be levelheaded like his dad. He was a busy student, and Steven saw him only occasionally when Jason could fit him in between his studies, part-time job, and friends. He knew Jason loved him, but at twenty he was enjoying life on his own with friends and roommates, and his priorities were his own. He often missed appointments they made, just forgetting about them. Steven felt that leaving him with his independence for a while was the best thing.

He was now deep in the trailer park. The trailers back here were newer than the ones up front. At the entrance the trailers looked fenced in with little patches of grass, as though they were trying to be houses with permanence. Back here they looked ready to leave on a moment's notice. Trailer 48 on the left, and it was 7:28. He was fine.

Debra had seemed friendly on the phone, the opposite of John. She told him that John had received similar calls over the years and had developed a method for handling them. Sometimes he saved the "fuck off" until after he hung up on them, sometimes not. But she always felt sorry for them and had called a few of them back, as she had done with Steven. Her voice seemed full of pity. He quickly agreed to meet her that night, and she warned him not to come before John left for work.

Number 56. Seven-thirty, right on the dot. No car next to the trailer, but the lights were on. He pulled his car into the short driveway.

He couldn't be sure, but as he stepped out of the car he thought he saw people peeking through the blinds from neighboring trailers. *This is like living in a fishbowl*, he thought. He walked to the door and knocked. There was nothing outside except a few children's toys scattered around the cement slab that extended from the trailer to form a small porch.

This has to work, he thought. *I don't know what else I can try. She has to have some answers.*

Two

"Debra?"

"Hi, come in," Debra said, stepping back from the door. Steven stepped up twice into the trailer and was assaulted by the smell of cat urine.

"Well, have a seat over there," she said, motioning to a small couch that was half occupied by Walmart bags. Steven noticed how crammed the place was – stacks of papers, boxes, storage tubs. The living room held the couch and a television which was tuned to *Jeopardy*. Debra pulled a chair out from under a kitchen table about six feet away from Steven and sat. She lit a cigarette.

"I hope you don't mind if I smoke," she said. "It is my house."

"Of course. No, I don't mind," Steven said. "Thank you for calling me back."

"Well, as I said, John just doesn't want to have anything to do with it anymore. He's tired of it, and I understand. It's bad enough to lose your father let alone a suicide. Not to mention the shame. But I spent some time in that house, so I have some idea." She picked up a remote from the table and turned off the television.

Steven swallowed. The cat piss smell stuck in his throat. The cigarette smoke was preferable. "What did you hear there?" he asked.

"Hear? I never heard anything. It's what I felt. We'd go over to help Ben, John's dad. He was getting worse and worse, dying slowly. He had a nurse come in and visit him each day, but John was real close with him, and wanted to visit every day too. At first I would go with him, but after a while I stayed home. It got to be too much."

"I imagine watching him die would be difficult," Steven said.

"Well, yes, it was, but that wasn't the reason. I liked Ben. And I wanted to help. But every time I'd walk in that house, especially those last few weeks, it felt miserable. Not because Ben was dying," she paused. "It was something else. In the house with him. You could feel it in the air, like a thickness. Very dark, very evil."

Steven cleared his throat and adjusted a little on the couch. He was never comfortable when people brought up irrational things like the word evil, or the word God, or anything supernatural, and he was a little self-conscious of how he appeared to people when they did. He was sure they could see his reaction, his discomfort, and this bothered him. He noticed a few other things in the trailer: a cross over the door, little pictures of Jesus here and there. Religious tracts on the table next to the couch. His comfort level was falling rapidly.

"Oh, you don't believe, I take it?" Debra asked.

"It's that obvious?"

"Like I sprayed you with vinegar," she replied.

"I guess not. I mean, I respect that you do, and —"

"Yeah," she cut him off. "You don't gotta do that. You don't believe, that's fine, I don't care. I didn't used to believe either, so I know exactly how you feel."

"Something changed your mind?"

"Yeah," she snorted. "That house." She stood and crushed her cigarette. "Look, I'm gonna tell you the same things I told the other two who came to see John about that place. And I can't pretend it was something it wasn't. There's something seriously wrong with that house. And I don't mean it's built wrong, or the electric don't work right. It's an evil in the air inside, you can feel it. And it's still there. I felt it even after Ben died. If there's anything that qualifies in your book as evil, you need to apply it to that house." She walked to the refrigerator. "You want something to drink? I got lemonade or beers."

"A beer would be nice."

Debra pulled two beers, popped one for Steven, and handed him the can. She sat back down and started another cigarette. Steven took a sip and asked, "You never saw anything? Heard anything, like knocking?"

"Never heard any knocking. But I didn't need to. The sound of Ben gasping for air was enough to send chills down your spine, make you realize how awful dying can be. All you had to do was look at him to know something was wrong. The doctors couldn't figure it out. They tested him for everything, but in the end they said he just lost his will to live, that's what was causing him to deteriorate, to kill himself," she scoffed.

"You don't think that was true?" Steven asked.

"Mister, he took a spoon from the kitchen drawer and gouged out his eyes before he killed himself. Bet the real estate agent didn't tell you about *that*," she said, flicking an ash into the tray beside her. "Does that sound like depression to you?"

"Maybe. Or maybe psychosis," Steven replied.

"Or maybe there was something he didn't want to see anymore," she said, becoming a little irritated. "Something that drove him to blind himself, so he wouldn't have to see it. And when that didn't end it, he took a steak knife from the same drawer and cut through his own throat. And I'll tell you something. Ben wasn't crazy at the end. At that point he knew what he was doing. No dementia, no weird behavior, nothing like that. You could tell. The longer I stayed in that house, visiting him, the more I understood it. It didn't surprise me that he did it."

"Honestly, that seems a little crazy," Steven said. "I mean, I understand how the doctors would think that."

This approach didn't seem to sit very well with Debra. She stood again, this time a little more quickly. "Listen, I've told you. I've warned you, that's what I felt I should do when you called, 'cause I know what that house is like and I'm sympathetic, even if John isn't. So there, I've done right by you. Whether or not you believe me is up to you, but I've done my part, told you what I thought you should know. So I guess we're done now." She moved toward the door.

Steven stood, a little surprised at the sudden end to the discussion. He regretted that his rationality clashed enough with her superstition that it was angering her, but he didn't know any other way to approach it, and it seemed she didn't have much else to offer. He sat the beer down on the table next to hers and followed her. She opened the door for him, and he stepped through.

"Look, if I've offended you, I'm very..."

"I'm not offended, I'm just not very patient. What are you gonna do?" she asked him as he stepped down to the cement slab.

"I don't know what I'm going to do," he replied.

She sighed. "Listen, do you have a priest, or a pastor?"

"No," he replied. "I don't go to church."

"That's too bad," she said, grabbing the door handle. "It's like they said in the movie. You're gonna need a bigger boat."

Then she shut the door.

Three

Thanks to Seattle traffic, Steven arrived home an hour later. During the drive he had plenty of time to think about what Debra had to say, which seemed damn little. It was hard to analyze something you didn't take seriously. He'd been hoping she might have once heard her father-in-law comment on the house, something that might have given him a direction to pursue, but instead all he got was "evil." Evil was for the irrational, the superstitious, and the simple minded. Steven was none of these things, and evil held little meaning for him.

Still, she didn't seem like a crackpot, the Jesus pictures aside. Most people who believed in religion weren't crackpots, Steven felt, just misguided. And he had no doubt she sincerely believed what she was saying. He just felt there must be more simple explanations. Evil was too handy a catch-all for the unexplained. It was just as likely the knockings were hallucinations on his part, and seeing a doctor to rule out a brain tumor might be a step he'd have to consider.

He pulled into his driveway and walked to the basement door. Once he threw the deadbolt and pushed it open he felt a stab of concern. The familiar buzzing of the house alarm didn't go off – he was sure he had armed it before he left. He walked to the keypad where he would normally punch in a code to disarm the alarm, and it was dead – no readout. Perhaps the electricity was off? No, lights were on next door. Light was shining down the stairwell that led up to the kitchen, from a light he always left on when away.

Steven felt his heart rate pick up. *Someone is, or was, in the house,* he thought. *Somehow they shut down the alarm system. I've probably been robbed...or am being robbed.* He contemplated quietly searching the house, but felt unarmed – what would he do if he ran into someone? Considering his options, he decided to announce himself. He walked back over to the basement door, opened it, and slammed it shut loud enough to wake the neighbors.

In response, there were footsteps above him, moving rapidly. *Fuck, they're upstairs right now,* he thought. Steven reached for his cell phone and dialed 911.

◊

"Nothing," said the second cop, returning from downstairs to the kitchen where Steven and the first cop stood. The first cop was filling out some paperwork. He spoke while he wrote.

"No forced entry. Are you sure you set the alarm? Sometimes people forget, more often than you realize."

"I'm almost positive I set it," Steven replied.

"You could have the alarm company run a test, see if everything is working properly," the cop replied.

"But the footsteps? I heard someone up here," Steven said.

"If there was someone here they're gone now," said the second cop.

"If?" Steven asked.

"Look," the first cop said, "you did the right thing calling us. I'm sure you heard something. You told us you slammed the door downstairs. They probably left through the front door as soon as you alerted them to your presence."

"I found the front door bolted," said Steven. "They didn't go out that way."

"We've checked the entire house and yard. I assure you there's no one here. My advice is to get your alarm fixed right away, and if anything else happens, call 911 again."

"Thanks," Steven said, resigned. He could tell this was routine for them, and they weren't going to make a case out of something they didn't need to, something they felt was most likely his mistake.

Steven made his own rounds through the house, double checking the bolts on the basement door, the kitchen door, and the front door. He checked all of the window locks, ensuring they held. He checked every closet. He even poked his head up into the attic and shined a flashlight into every corner until he was sure he was alone.

It's difficult to sleep in a house you believe has just been robbed or invaded. Steven knew he had heard footsteps overhead when he slammed the basement door. Could the footsteps have been some kind of echo? If someone had been upstairs, where did they go? If this ended with the same explanation as the knocking – no explanation – it was going to drive him crazy.

It's likely I'm not thinking straight about this, he thought. *Better sleep and see how things look in the morning. Daylight will bring a fresh perspective.*

Steven climbed into bed but sleep was not forthcoming. There were too many ideas floating around in his head, and too much adrenaline in his system. Every idea he proposed for the sound of the footsteps didn't stick – nothing seemed like a reasonable answer. He felt as if he were going around and around, trying out the same ideas over and over, but not finding an answer each time.

He continued running scenarios through his mind for a long time before he drifted off.

◊

Steven awoke to the sound of knocking. He strained his ears, threw his legs out of the bed, and stumbled into the hallway, listening. He was trying to discern the direction of the follow-up knocks which were sure to come. They always did.

Then four more knocks, just like before. From downstairs. But then, unlike previous nights, more sounds. A shuffling, like someone walking.

He struggled with his balance as his body attempted to wake up. He walked to the top of the stairs, and looked down into the basement. The light at the foot of the stairs was dim, coming from the moonlight in an adjacent basement window. Steven strained to focus his eyes which were blurry with sleep. The house was silent now, and he strained his ears for any sound of movement, something that would tell him what was happening. For several moments he stood there like an animal, defenses up, senses strained to detect a threat. His eyes continued to adjust to the darkness, and he looked for anything in the pattern of the moonlight that might indicate to him the source of the sound. Then he saw it. It passed almost imperceptibly from left to right at the base of the stairs. They were in the house again. He considered calling 911, then dismissed it. *What am I going to tell them?* he thought. *That I saw a shadow? I need to know what I'm dealing with.*

He felt sweat break out, and he rubbed his eyes. He focused again. No movement, but now he heard the sound of water running. It was coming from downstairs.

He walked down slowly and quietly. He was scared, but he was also determined to find out who was inside the house. He considered turning on the stairwell light, then decided not to. This time he wouldn't scare them away. Perhaps whoever was in the house didn't realize he was awake, and he felt this gave him an advantage.

At the base of the stairs he turned right and entered a hallway that led to a bathroom where the sound of water was coming from. The door to the bathroom was open, and as he approached the door he heard the sound of the faucet being twisted off. The water stopped, followed by a few drips. Steven was convinced he'd cornered them, there was no way out of the bathroom. Time to confront whatever was there.

He stepped in and turned on the light. He could smell the slight chlorine odor of freshly run water. The shower curtain to the oversize tub was pulled back, and in the tub stood about six inches of water. He glanced around the room – no one was there. The room had no closets or corners where someone could hide. He walked over to the tub and looked down into the water, searching for some explanation, something to make sense of what he was seeing. He reached down into the tub to pull up the stopper. To his shock it was already up. The water wasn't draining. *It must be plugged for some reason*, he thought. *Yes, it's plugged, that explains it, and there's been a slow drip that I haven't noticed, and it's been accumulating for hours.* He knew this didn't explain the sounds he'd heard or the movement he'd seen, but this partial explanation accounted for the water, and he was willing to go with it for now.

Determined to figure out what was blocking the drain, he leaned over the tub and dug his fingers into the holes on the sides of the stopper, searching for the blockage.

With his face just inches from the sides of the tub, he heard it again – four knocks. This time coming from overhead, behind him. Instinctively he twisted his neck to look up, but as he did so, a large drop of liquid hit his face and it caused him to flinch. With one hand in the drain and the other trying to prop himself up, he lost his stability and fell face-first into the water, its chill jolting awake any parts of his body still asleep. He pushed himself up with his arms and lifted his head from the water, wiping his face. His hand came away bloody. *Great, I've cut myself*, he thought. Then he heard the knocking again, directly above him. The sensation that someone was in the room with him washed over him like the coldness of the water. He knew it was above him, behind him. In his mind he couldn't rationalize how it could be above him in the tub, but he knew it was there, just as you know when someone is standing behind you even though you haven't seen them. At first he felt too frightened to turn to face it, but he realized that for his own sanity he needed to get an answer, to see what he was dealing with. He could hear his heartbeat pounding in the blood in his ears. He turned over onto his back to see what was above him.

Something was there, moving, but at first he couldn't make it out. Nothing was distinct. It was as though it was forming, coming together. After a few seconds it had enough shape that Steven could see it was the head of an old man with his eyes closed. There were deep wrinkles in the face, and wisps of the man's hair drifted above his head. It floated slowly, moving back and forth in a gentle way. Steven was stunned at the image, almost mesmerized by it. He felt like an animal being hypnotized before a kill.

It began to move towards him. He noticed the man's neck – it was roughly severed, ragged, dripping blood, which fell onto Steven. Trying to keep some distance from it, Steven lowered his body back towards the water in the tub as the head approached him. The image of the man kept shifting, like it was behind panes of old glass. When it was about a foot away from his face, the eyes opened, revealing sockets filled with blood that began to run down the man's cheeks.

Reflexes caused Steven to throw his head backwards and he hit the back of his head against the bottom of the tub. Water rushed in over his face and for a moment he felt he was drowning. He could feel his heart beating out of his chest. He reached out again to the sides of the tub, trying to grab hold, but his hands were wet and slippery with the combination of water and blood. The image was right above him now, just above the surface of the water. If he raised up, he'd hit it with his head. He felt trapped. He hadn't managed to suck in much air before he went under, and he was feeling the need to breathe. He flailed his arms against the side of the tub, reaching for the upper edge on the left side to pull himself up. He flung his right arm over his torso to reach for the left edge, and grabbing it, pulled with all of his might. He felt himself roll out and slip onto the cold tile of the bathroom floor. There was a sharp pain in his right knee when his leg crashed from the edge of the tub onto the floor. He turned his body to look at the head, to see if it was still coming at him.

It was gone.

He quickly inspected his body, looking for a cut or a gash. He felt the back of his head. There was no blood, not coming from him, or in the water. The water in the tub was crystal clear, just as it looked when he entered the room.

Lying on the floor, he grabbed a towel and wiped it over his face. He was breathing hard and his body was shaking from the cold water. He closed his eyes, rolled onto his back, and tried to take several deep breaths. He could hear the water draining from the tub, as though he had just finished a bath. He felt his heartbeat slowly return to a normal rhythm, and he felt the need to get up and dry off. But he was terrified to open his eyes while looking up. He rolled onto his side, knelt, and stood up, then opened them. The room looked normal, no water in the tub, and everything in its place, except his ability to make sense of what had just happened.

Four

Steven waited in the small office for the doctor to come back. *Thank god for COBRA,* he thought. After the event last night, Steven had stayed up trying to understand it. The only rational explanation was a brain tumor or some disorder that was causing him to hallucinate. The knocking, the footsteps, and now the incident in the bathtub – they all had to be hallucinations. He had just listened, hours before, to Debra's story of how Ben had committed suicide. It wasn't a big leap to think his brain, if it was sick, had taken that story and ran with it. And consistent with a brain tumor, the hallucinations were getting worse. This explanation made sense and it was almost a relief. *If having a brain tumor can be considered a relief,* he thought.

The doctor came into the room and shut the door behind him. "Listen Steven, the neurological tests are all negative. I can't say I see anything that would indicate a tumor. We could do an MRI but I'm not sure that would help." He tapped his pen on the folder he held. "Describe the hallucinations to me again."

Steven recounted the knocking and footsteps. When he described the head, he left out most of the gory details.

He didn't want the doctor to think he was completely batshit. A floating, disembodied head was good enough for diagnosis. He didn't want to wind up in an asylum for christsake.

"Yeah, that's pretty severe," the doctor said.

"I know how crazy it sounds, but that's why I'm here. Something like a tumor is an explanation that makes sense. I'm sane enough to know there's a rational explanation."

The doctor kept flipping through the paperwork. "Do you take any drugs?"

"Only the ones you've prescribed for me," Steven replied.

"Just the Lozol, nothing else?"

"I'm not a drug abuser, if that's where you're headed."

"No, I'm just looking for combinations that might result in something like this," the doctor replied.

"No. Nothing other than the Lozol."

"Anything for pain?"

"Ibuprofen, aspirin. Rarely."

"How are you sleeping?"

"Not well. I never wake up feeling good."

"I notice you didn't put down any next of kin. Are all of your family passed away?"

"No, I should have put my father, but he doesn't like me to list him for anything without him knowing about it in advance. He's a little particular that way."

"Well, why don't you arrange that with him and call my staff back with the contact info. I have to have some kind of next of kin listed for DNR and that kind of thing. Do you know of any health conditions your father or mother have had? Anything like this?"

"My mother passed away after dementia years ago, but that was just caused by old age, right? She was seventy two. Nothing in my father's history that I know of. Or their parents. But people of their generation were very secretive about anything, you know, mental, so one of them might have had issues and just never told anyone."

The doctor paused. "When did you say the hallucinations first started?"

"About two months ago. Very minor back then, nothing like last night."

"What happened in your life two months ago?"

"Well, I moved into a new house. And I was let go."

The doctor flipped the folder closed. "Those are two of the biggest stressors people have in their lives. Only divorce and death in the family rank higher. You've had two big ones within a few weeks of each other. It's most likely that stress is the cause."

"Really?" This seemed too simple, but then, the doctor was the expert. And it *was* an explanation.

"Yes, trust me. I'll prescribe a sedative for you. You said you've had difficulty sleeping, that's probably compounding it. Lack of sleep can lead to all kinds of strange things. I want you to find ways to reduce stress, get plenty of rest, and take this sedative just before bedtime each night for the next two weeks. Schedule an appointment with me two weeks out and we'll see how things stand. If things have improved, great. If not, we'll see about an MRI." The doctor handed Steven the prescription, and before he could ask another question, opened the door, and was off to the next patient in the room next door.

◊

"You look like hell!"

Steven stared back at the old man in the doorway. "You too," he replied.

The old man's lips cracked into a smile. "Come on in."

Steven entered the house he grew up in. Familiar pictures hung on the walls, and forty year old furniture graced the living room. It had a particular smell, too. It made him feel three feet tall. Roy, his father, motioned for him to sit. The chair used to be covered in plastic, back when his mother was alive. Roy had removed the plastic after she died.

"What's up?"

"Listen, I was at the doctor's today, and they insist on having a next of kin listing. I don't want to list Jason, and god knows I'm not going to give them Sheryl's name. So it has to be you."

His dad got up, agitated. "What about Bernie? He'd do it."

"He lives in San Antonio. You're right here."

"I don't like being on lists."

"I know," Steven said. His dad's stubbornness on this issue really got under his skin, especially since it was in the interest of Steven's health. Most fathers would have said "sure" without a second thought. Not Roy.

"This is a private medical listing, they'd only call you if there was some medical emergency involving me. They can't disclose your name or contact info without getting sued. Medical records are very private."

"Private my ass. If they're so private, why's my Medicare premium so high?" he yelled back from the kitchen.

Steven sighed. "They're high for everyone. Medical costs have been skyrocketing the last thirty years, ever since Nixon and HMOs."

"Don't you bring up Nixon."

He could have and he normally would have continued discussing medical costs, but Steven retreated, knowing he was going down the wrong path. It was easy to get sidetracked when talking with Roy; it was a pattern they had engaged in for years. They both had the ability to bait each other into discussions neither really wanted to have and that always ended badly. He needed to get back to the point.

"Look, I need this favor, so please do it for me, OK? I guarantee you won't be bothered unless something serious happens to me. If it does, I'd rather you make decisions for me, not Jason, not Bernie. OK? By the way, who do you have listed with your doctors as next of kin now that Mom's gone?"

Roy ignored the question and returned from the kitchen with a beer in hand. "I won't do it unless you tell me what's going on."

"What do you mean?" Steven asked.

"Something's going on. You look like hell, you've gone to the doctor about it, and you look as worried as a Catholic on his way to confession. Out with it."

Steven sighed. Whenever Roy wanted some information, it was easier to give it to him than to resist. "I may have a brain tumor."

"You don't have a brain tumor," Roy said.

"Thanks for your sympathy, Dad."

"What makes you think that?"

"I've been seeing and hearing things. Things that aren't there."

"What did the doctor say about it?"

"He ran some neurological tests, all negative. He says it's stress."

"Damn doctors wouldn't know their asshole from a hole in the ground."

"It makes sense," Steven replied. "Moving to the new house, losing my job."

"What kinda things?" Roy asked.

"What?"

"What kind of things have you been seeing, that aren't there?"

"Well, it started with knockings," Steven answered. "I would wake up at night, convinced I'd heard someone knocking. It's been happening since I moved into the new house. It happens every night."

"Plumbing?" asked Roy.

"Replaced it all with PEX. It isn't the plumbing," Steven replied.

"Neighbor kids?"

"I set up a webcam to monitor the yard – nothing."

"What's a webcam?"

"Surveillance. A video camera that's triggered when there's motion. A cat came by, but that was it. It's not kids."

"You think it's something supernatural," Roy said, looking at Steven.

"No, of course not. It's a brain tumor."

"You do, and you don't want to admit it. There's something you're not telling me."

Steven sighed. "Last night I had a severe hallucination. Saw the head of a man, the man who killed himself in my house fifteen years ago. It scared the hell out of me. That's why I went to the doctor."

Roy sat his beer down, and gave him a look Steven remembered from his youth that meant *how stupid are you?*

"Your new house is a death house?" Roy said. "You moved into a goddamn death house?"

"Please. Every house is a death house, people die in homes all the time."

"Yeah," Roy replied, "but you don't know about it. It's the knowing that gets you. You knew about this one, how'd you know?"

Steven told him about Ben and about his trip to the trailer park to speak with Debra.

Roy looked stunned. "I just cannot figure out why a child of mine would want to move into a house where someone committed suicide."

"Dad, it's done. It's completely irrational to not buy a house for that reason."

"And now you're here telling me you have a brain tumor. Look at you. You're always two steps removed from what's really happening. You have been your whole life. The only thing wrong with you is that you're too goddamn stubborn to realize you're living in a haunted house."

"Dad, you know how insane that sounds."

"Not as insane as you choosing to live in it."

Steven paused. This was going nowhere. He should just finalize the next of kin thing and go. But his dad's immediate willingness to believe in the idea of a haunted house actually surprised him. He always assumed his dad would be skeptical of those kinds of things. His mother had been religious – extremely religious – but his dad had always stayed home from church, didn't participate in the church activities that his mother insisted the rest of the family participate in, and Steven had always interpreted it as his father sharing his lack of belief in anything supernatural. But maybe he was wrong. Maybe he did believe.

Or maybe he just hated going to church. *God knows I did*, Steven thought.

Steven remembered something his brother Bernard had told him when they were kids, playing a game of Battleship. Bernie had just won a game and they were setting up for another. What Steven had always remembered was Bernie's comment: "Don't ever play with Dad. He knows where the ships are, no matter what you do." He hadn't asked Bernie what he meant by it, because he knew what it meant, but it made him uncomfortable and he changed the subject. He remembered thinking at the time that Bernie knew Roy had some kind of ability that they never discussed, and he had no interest in knowing more about it. Now Steven decided to open that door a little and see if it was true, if it was what he thought it was years ago.

"I need another favor," Steven asked. "I need someone to see what I've seen, or hear what I've heard. If someone else can see or hear it too, then I'll know it's not a brain tumor, that I'm not going crazy. And if that's true, then you won't have to have your name listed at my doctor's office as next of kin."

"What do you want me to do?" Roy asked.

"I want you to spend the night at my house, in the guest bedroom. If nothing happens, fine. But if the knocking comes back, at least I won't be the only one who's heard it. Maybe you can help me get a handle on what's going on. I know…that you can do that." Steven glanced at Roy to see if he had picked up on what he meant.

Roy seemed to be mulling it over. "You want me to spend a night with you in your haunted house?"

Steven smiled a little. "Yes, Dad. A night in the haunted house. Just like a grade school dare."

Roy looked down at his hands, then chuckled softly, almost to himself. "It was so goddamn boring around here the past few years since Claire died. There were times I'd stare at the wallpaper, trying to think of something interesting to do. A ghost hunt sounds like just the thing. I'm in."

Five

Steven returned to pick up Roy at nine p.m. The ten minute trip back to Steven's house was peppered with banal updates from Roy about the neighbor's dog and a problem with the gas bill. Steven normally did not spend much time with Roy – they had never been close as father and son, even while he was growing up. Now they seemed to have a mutually acceptable arrangement of seeing each other twice a year, once during the holidays and once during a summer BBQ that Roy's brother held each Fourth of July. But other than that, even though they lived only a few miles apart, they rarely communicated. Steven wasn't used to talking with him for much more than a couple of minutes at a time. He was going to have to try harder if he wanted his help.

He pulled the car into his driveway and he and Roy walked into the basement. The alarm had inexplicably started working again, and Steven disarmed it. He turned to his father and pointed overhead.

"This is where I heard the footsteps last night when I got home. I came in the door and the alarm wasn't working. I thought someone might be home, so to scare them I decided to slam the door closed, thinking they'd run."

"Damn fool idea."

Steven ignored him. "As soon as the door closed I heard the footsteps upstairs. They were unmistakable. So I called 911."

"Another damn fool idea."

Steven sighed, irritated. "If you think someone is in the house," he said to Roy, "most people would call the cops."

"Nothing wrong with the cops," Roy replied. "But it's stupid to think they can do anything about ghosts."

Steven didn't know how to reply to this.

"Where do you keep your guns?" Roy asked.

"I don't have a gun."

Roy looked at Steven as though he was from outer space. "Well don't you think that might be a good idea, with people breaking into your house?"

"Well, you can't shoot a ghost," Steven shot back.

It seemed like a stalemate, and neither of them spoke for a moment. The longer things were silent, the more Steven felt like he should apologize.

"Dad, listen, I —"

"It's your story," Roy cut him off, waving a hand. "Keep talking."

OK, back on track, Steven thought, then continued. "I never found anyone inside. The cops searched the place. No forcible entry, they don't know how they got in. The front door and the kitchen door are the only ways out up there, and they were both bolted when I went up. If they went out a window, they bothered to lock the window from the inside on their way out. I think the cops thought I imagined it."

Roy contemplated this. Steven expected him to say something sarcastic but instead he just seemed to be thinking. "Then what?" Roy asked.

"Well, I tried to go to bed. Took forever to get to sleep, I was too wired by the idea that someone had broken in. I woke up around 3 a.m. Heard the knocking."

"What did it sound like?"

Steven walked to the wall and knocked on it four times. "Well, kind of like that. It sounds more muffled, like it's coming from a room on the other side of the house. Then it happened again, a second time, maybe ten or fifteen seconds later – four more knocks. When it first started weeks ago I thought it was coming from the front door, but I ruled that out. It was coming from somewhere inside the house, one of the interior walls. That's when I thought it might be the plumbing. But it's still happening, every night – and it seems to move – it doesn't come from the same place every night."

"Hmmff," Roy snorted.

"Then last night," Steven continued, "it happened again. I got up during the pause between the knocks. It seemed to be coming from downstairs. When I looked down the stairwell, I thought I saw movement and I heard the sound of water running."

"That's when you went into the bathroom?" Roy asked.

"Yes," Steven said, leading Roy around the hallway and into the downstairs bathroom so he could reference the layout there. "The tub had water in it but wasn't running. The drain was open, but the water wouldn't drain. I knelt over it to see if something was blocking it, and that's when I felt the blood. Hit me on the back of the head. You know the rest."

Roy stepped over to the tub. "So there was a head floating," he held his arm out, pointing into the space above the tub, under the shower head, "...right here?"

"Well, no, it was more over here, in the middle, but yes, it was there, floating. Staring down at me."

Roy yanked his hand away from where he was pointing, a look of pain on his face. He rubbed the hand with his other, wincing.

"What?" Steven asked. "Did you feel something?"

"Yeah, I think it bit me."

Steven rushed over to his dad, wanting to help but not knowing how. "Are you OK?" he asked.

Roy dropped his arms. "Yeah, I'm just fucking with ya," he said, and smiled.

Steven dropped his head, relieved, but pissed. "Look, I'm trying to —"

"Lighten up!" Roy said, and walked out of the room. Steven could hear him going upstairs.

Between the ghosts and his father, it was going to be a long night.

◊

Steven awoke in a panic, his heart racing. He had just woken from a familiar nightmare he had experienced several times since moving into the house. In the nightmare he had fallen into a lake, drowning. He would swim to the surface, but upon reaching it he would suddenly be five feet deeper and would have to swim to the surface again. It had gone on and on like this until he thought his lungs would burst and his arms give out. The dream was filled with despair and hopelessness; a sense that he would never reach the surface, that there was no point of trying to survive. He sat up in bed, his senses returning, and sucked in the bedroom's air in large gasping breaths. After a moment he started to breathe normally, and checked the clock on the nightstand: 12:34. He could hear his father snoring in the bedroom next door.

He rubbed his face with his hands. *Get a grip, just a nightmare*, he thought. *Think about something else and try to go back to sleep. Like you've done a hundred times whenever you've had a nightmare.*

The light from the clock was very dim, but it lit his room just enough to be able to make out the dresser, some artwork on the walls, and the closet door. *Most people have no idea what their bedrooms look like at night, in the dark,* he thought. *Maybe insomniacs, or the crazy, or the haunted. Most people have their eyes closed once they turn off the light, so they're not aware of all the little lights and shadows that exist in a bedroom at night.* All the ones he noticed in his bedroom now seemed new to him, and unnerving. He had just resigned himself to sliding back down into bed and giving sleep another chance when he saw it.

It was very faint, in the corner of the room. He strained his eyes, pinching them closed a little in an attempt to focus.

A pale, white face. Barely visible. Small, like a child, about the same height as the bed. Staring at him.

A chill went up his spine. His first reaction was to freeze, an animal instinct to camouflage himself.

It knows I've seen it, he thought.

He strained his eyes and instead of pinching them to focus, widened them to let in as much light as possible. There was no question it was the face of a small boy. It wasn't moving or reacting; it just stared at him. He thought he could just make out all of the facial features – eyes, nose, cheeks, chin – no ears. It was faint – it looked like a dimly lit painting, and when he stared at it too hard, it almost seemed to fade out.

Maybe it's a reflection of light from the window, he thought. *Wouldn't be the first time I've scared myself with a shadow.* He shifted his eyes to the bedroom window, trying to find something that would account for the image. *Maybe I'm still dreaming?* he thought. It didn't feel like he was dreaming, but then, it never does in a dream. He was afraid to return his eyes to the face, but he forced himself to do it. It was still there, still staring. It had to be some kind of reflection that he was misinterpreting.

Then it blinked.

He gasped. Instantly his curiosity turned to fear. *There's someone in the room,* he thought. *Why is he just standing there? What is he going to do?*

Steven sat frozen, staring at the face in the corner. He didn't dare remove his gaze from it, in fear it might move within the room and he lose track of it, which would be much worse. The longer he stared at it, the more he began to feel or sense the presence in the room and the more frightened he became.

Then he became aware in his peripheral vision of something to the left. He let his gaze shift away from the face, and there, in the other corner of the room, another face. Just as dim and pale. This one was a little higher and the features looked like a girl. He looked back to the right and the first face was still there, lifeless and cold, not moving. But they were definitely staring right at him. They looked like death masks with open eyes, floating in the air.

When the next face appeared at the foot of his bed, he involuntarily pulled up his legs, horrified. It was just above the height of the bed, not more than three feet off the ground. It was a different face than the others, rounder and smaller, and it stared directly at him with the same lifeless intensity. Now he felt cornered, under attack.

When the fourth face appeared next to the nightstand, he'd had enough. He reached for the light on the nightstand, and switched it on.

All of the faces were gone.

Of course they're gone, he thought. *Ghosts don't like light.*

He scanned the room for something that might explain the faces – something he'd changed recently? The curtain on the window was shut tight – no moonlight came in. Reflections from the clock light perhaps? Then why did they appear one after the other?

And it blinked, he thought. *It definitely blinked.*

Shaken, he got out of bed, threw on a robe, and quietly walked to the guest room. His father was still snoring. *There was no way I could have shown him that,* Steven thought, *and they're gone now anyway.* He decided to let him sleep. Perhaps the knocking would return, like it had every night around three. He'd be able to rouse his dad for that, when it came.

A cold breeze hit his left arm, and Steven turned to look down the dim hallway. There, at the end of it, a shadow against the wall. There was enough ambient light in the house to easily walk around between rooms if you knew the layout, and shadows were everywhere, just like they are in every house at night. This shadow, however, had the shape of a man, about Steven's height, with a slightly distended head. Steven froze with the same reaction as the faces, again afraid that someone was in the house. *If it's just a shadow, it won't move*, he thought. *Let's just watch it until I'm sure...*

He remained frozen, staring at the shadow, trying not to blink, afraid he might miss a movement. It seemed motionless, and the longer Steven stared at it the more convinced he became that it must be caused by something innocent, something else he wasn't registering. He remained frozen, continuing to stare. It had been at least a minute, no movement. That was long enough, wasn't it? He would walk down to the end of the hall and see what was creating the shadow, and be done with it. It hadn't moved, so it must be benign.

Then things shifted, a tiny amount. Almost imperceptible. It looked like the shadow was coming apart, holes growing in it. Two slits in the head that slowly enlarged. After a few seconds they stopped growing. Steven knew what they were even before the pupils appeared – eyes.

Steven grabbed the door handle to Roy's room. "Roy, wake up." He walked into the room and shook his father. He grabbed his shoulders to practically lift him out of bed.

Roy stumbled as Steven led him out the door, and pointed to the end of the hall. "Look," he whispered.

Roy rubbed his head, trying to wake up. It took him a moment to focus, but then he saw it.

"Shit," Roy said.

"Can you believe that?" Steven whispered.

Both of them observed the pupils in the eyes at the end of the hall shift to look at Roy.

"Shit!" Roy said again.

Then the shadow began to move down the hall towards them. The eyes remained fixed on Roy. As it approached, it slowly descended, disappearing into the floor as though it was walking down an invisible flight of stairs. Steven and Roy took a step back when it was still six feet away, but now no more than the top of the head still appeared. Another second and it was gone.

The two stood in the hallway, unsure of what to say or do next.

"Every fucking hair on my neck is standing up," Roy said.

"It was looking at you," Steven said.

"Yeah," Roy replied. "That's the creepiest goddamn thing I've seen in a long time."

◊

Steven told Roy about the faces he'd seen earlier in his bedroom. They discussed having a cup of coffee, but it was still before 1 a.m. and opted instead to try and return to sleep, to see if more would occur. Steven mentioned that they still hadn't heard the knocking that occurred every night, and that it usually happened around 3 a.m. Both Steven and Roy retired to their rooms and tried to get back to sleep.

Steven looked at the bottle of sedatives that the doctor had prescribed for him, sitting on his nightstand. *Not tonight,* he thought. *I'll start them tomorrow, but tonight I need to make sure Dad hears the knocking, and I'm not sure how heavy he sleeps.*

After a half hour of replaying the occurrences of the evening in his mind, Steven's eyes finally closed and he drifted off.

◊

Old faithful, Steven thought, as he swung his feet to the floor and stood, preparing to walk into his father's room, even before the final rap of the first series of four had ended. The clock read 3:09.

He turned the corner into the hallway and approached the guest room. They had about fifteen seconds before the second series of knockings would come, and he wanted his dad to be fully awake to hear them.

But as he opened the door to the guest bedroom he realized something was wrong. Something was in the room with Roy, he could feel it. He scanned the room quickly, still wanting to wake his father, but feeling he should identify what was wrong first. He took a step into the room and saw it – the shadow, and the eyes. They were staring down at

Roy as he slept. The eyes were floating in mid-air, inside the shadow, which was in the middle of the room. It seemed to be pulsing, at times vivid and pronounced but then fading and becoming indistinct. It didn't seem to care that he had entered the room, it just kept staring at Roy.

Steven called to his father to wake up while watching the eyes to see if they would react. They didn't. His dad didn't respond; Steven called again. He shifted his gaze to his father, and Steven saw for the first time that something was wrong with him. His body was as stiff as a board, shaking very slightly, and – he blinked his eyes to be sure – hovering about an inch off the bed.

It seemed to Steven that his father was under some kind of attack, that the shadow figure was doing something to him. He heard the first knock of the second series. It was much louder than he'd ever heard it before, it seemed to be coming from everywhere. Now he wasn't worried about his father hearing the knocking, he was worried that the shadow was harming him, maybe even killing him. No longer concerned about the eyes or his own safety, he rushed to his father's side, grabbing his shoulders.

"Wake up, Dad!" he said as he shook Roy. "Wake up, for god's sake!" It seemed that every muscle in Roy's body was contracted. Shaking his shoulders caused Roy's whole body to move. He looked at Roy's closed eyes, waiting for them to open, but Roy was unresponsive. He heard the second knock, as loud as the first and lasting longer than normal, as though the sound itself was in slow motion. He felt under his father, confirming there was space there, enough for him to slide his hand entirely under his father's body. He glanced back over his shoulder to see if the shadow was still there, and yes, the eyes still hovered in the same position, now staring at both Roy and Steven.

Steven knew he had to do something. "Let him go!" Steven yelled. He stood from the side of the bed and approached the shadow, more angry than scared. He didn't have any idea what he was going to do once he reached it, but it felt like his only option. The third knock resounded in the distance and the eyes in the shadow shifted now to look at Steven. Steven froze. The eyes looked human, but they were off, not quite right. He sensed malevolence, the kind of feeling you sometimes get when you read about something abhorrent and repugnant. *This thing is evil,* he thought. *There's no other word for it.* His body felt freezing cold and a wave of despair washed over him that made him want to drop to his knees in defeat. He forced himself to take another step toward it, and as he approached within an arm's length, the eyes closed, leaving only the black of the shadow, which began to move away from him. He felt the cold and hopelessness diminish. He watched it drift towards the bedroom door, as though it was walking out of the room. He followed it, and once again he saw it descend into the floor of the hallway as the fourth knock hit and reverberated throughout the house.

He rushed back to his father, who now was lying firmly on the bed. He grabbed his shoulders again, to give him a gentle shaking. He could tell instantly that the muscles were now relaxed, like they should be. Roy's eyes opened and then winced in pain. "Goddamn," he complained, looking at Steven.

"Are you hurt? Do I need to call an ambulance?" Steven asked.

"No ambulance, no," Roy replied, wincing again. "I feel like I've been hit by a truck."

"Can you sit up?" Steven asked.

Roy tried, and found himself able, though certain movements surprised him with pain. "I could really use a couple aspirin or something," he said.

"What hurts?" Steven asked.

"Everything hurts," Roy replied.

"Stay there, I'll bring you some." Steven walked into the hallway and down to the bathroom, retrieving a couple of pills and a glass of water. He waited while his father swallowed them and drank the water. "I heard the knocking, and came in to get you. The shadow we saw in the hall earlier, it was in here with you."

Roy looked up at him.

"It had some kind of hold on you," Steven told him. "Your body was completely stiff, and…" Steven paused, becoming uncomfortable with the irrationality of what he was about to say.

"Yeah?" Roy asked. "What? Tell me."

"You were floating above the bed."

"Really?" Roy seemed intrigued, but Steven didn't know if it was sarcasm.

"Maybe it was something else, maybe it was due to your muscles spasming," Steven said.

Roy chuckled. "Even with all this, everything in the last few hours, you still think it's hallucinations?" Roy asked.

"I don't know what it is," Steven replied. "Yes, my mind looks for something normal to explain it."

"Oh, you're making my head hurt more. I need a cup of coffee. Make me some, OK?"

◊

Steven and Roy sat at the kitchen table. Each had a mug of strong coffee in their hands, drinking liberally. Roy asked a few more questions about what happened, and Steven filled him in.

"So," Roy asked, "you went at the shadow because you thought it was attacking me."

"Right. I couldn't get you to wake up and I could tell something was wrong with your body. You were as stiff as a board."

"That would explain why I feel worked over," Roy said.

"And it just left. Closed its eyes, drifted out into the hallway, and disappeared into the floor, just like earlier."

Roy spent a moment contemplating this. "I suppose there's something we should talk about," Roy said.

"Yeah?" Steven asked, almost dreading what his father was about to say.

"In my younger days, I used to be able to..." he paused, seeming to search for the right words. "I used to be able to feel things. I could pick up on things other people didn't seem to be able to feel or notice."

"What do you mean?" Steven asked, sensing he was about to hear what Bernie had referred to years ago. He felt uncomfortable.

"You know what I mean," Roy replied. "I know you know. You just hate admitting it."

"I'm not sure I do," Steven told him. "Maybe I do. But why don't you just tell me, so I don't have to guess."

Roy shook his head. "Always this way. You've always been this way, ever since you could speak. Always on the banks, but never with a pole in the water."

"What?" Steven asked. "What are you talking about?"

"Stevie, there's a wide river in front of you, rushing along, thousands and thousands of gallons of water moving every second, all coming from somewhere, all going somewhere. You can't see what's in there, but there are things in there, moving along with it. We both know that. You, because someone told you there's things in the river. You like to pretend they're not there. Me, I know they're there because I jump into it and find them, touch them, experience them."

Steven wasn't prepared to go along with it. It sounded too kooky. "A river?"

"Not a literal river, no. It's one that most people can't see or choose not to see. But it's there, moving, full of things. I found out when I was younger that I could jump into that river, swim in it. Find things. Come back out. When I told some people about it, it scared the hell out of them, but my father knew what I meant. He could do it too. He taught me to be selective in whom I told."

"I had no idea," Steven said. It was a lie, but he wanted to see where this was going.

"Your mother knew," Roy said. "She did not approve of it. There was an incident, early in our marriage, just after you were born. She got a glimpse of it. Scared her to death. I felt bad about it, tried to soothe her. I tried to explain it to her, make her understand it was nothing to be afraid of. But she was so jarred by it, so shaken, that she went the other way. Turned completely batshit Christian, made me swear to never do it, especially not around you. Or your bother, when he arrived. I agreed, partially because I knew I could still do it and she would never know, I just had to keep it secret from her. But I suppressed it for years and I think that created a sense of something being bottled up. Every year she got more and more churchy, dragging you boys off to bible-this and that, goddamn church camps and all, and it didn't matter what I had to say about it."

"I always wondered why you never came to church," Steven said.

"Did you like going to church?" Roy asked.

"God no," Steven said.

"Neither did I," Roy said, slapping the table. "Wasn't going to waste my time. But I think she felt that shoving Jesus down your throat would protect you from this other side of things. I think she was afraid one or both of you would...inherit it, and she was gonna build up defenses so it wouldn't take."

Steven considered this. Was Roy implying that Bernie, or himself, might have this same ability?

"What do you call it?" Steven asked. "This ability you have. Does it have a name?"

"I don't have a name for it," Roy replied. "And to be honest with you, I haven't dabbled in it much for a while. I got so tired of hiding it from Claire, I gave up after a while, it was just easier. She got really crazy about it in those last few years, I didn't dare mention it, it would send her into hours of crazy bible thumping. I think at the end she began to view me as the devil or something like that. Accused me of it more than once during the dementia. Then, after she passed, I considered cranking it back up, but I've not done much with it. One night after she was gone, when I was particularly lonely, I thought maybe I'd try to contact her – you know, from the other side."

Steven felt a lump in his throat, saddened that his dad had felt that lonely. He suddenly felt guilty for not visiting him more.

"But," Roy continued, "I didn't because I knew even if she could talk to me she never would that way, out of her hatred of it. She'd be too busy staring endlessly into the eyes of Jesus to bother and talk with me. Hell, I don't think we said a dozen words to each other that last year she was alive anyway. But I did miss her."

They sat in silence for a moment. Steven knew his mother's extreme religiousness was a big reason why he was such a rationalist now. It was pure rebellion, a one-eighty from what she hoped he would be. He hadn't considered his father also held beliefs he found just as unpalatable but were never expressed.

Roy stood and refilled his coffee mug. "Listen, I think you made your point. You're not crazy, there's no brain tumor. Something's going on here and it's taking a toll on you. Like I told you, you look like shit."

"It's because of sleep," Steven replied. "The knocking, every night."

"Fuck the knocking," Roy replied. "The knocking is just the appetizer. You got a real problem here. The knocking is just to wake you up so they can scare the shit out of you. And it's working, because they know you can't accept what you're seeing. Nothing more horrible than a brain tumor."

"They?" Steven asked. "Who is 'they'?"

Roy sat back down. "That's what we're going to find out."

"How?"

"Not sure just yet," Roy replied. "But I have some ideas. Drive me home. There's some things I need to do."

The early colors of dawn were just appearing in the sky. Steven sat down his coffee and went to look for his car keys.

Six

"This seems pointless, Dad," Steven said as he picked up his father once again at his house and drove him back to Steven's to spend another night. Steven had taken his father home earlier that morning and dropped him off. Later that afternoon he had received a call from Roy asking him to come and pick him up at 9 p.m., that he wanted to spend the night again. He told him that he wanted to hold a "trance" at the house, with his help. Steven felt it was a useless exercise.

"Tell me what this is and why we're doing it," Steven insisted.

"Your tone could use a little softening, considering I'm helping you here," Roy replied.

"Sorry, I don't mean to be rude, I just want to know what the plan is, and why you think it will matter."

"The plan," Roy said, "is a trance. I did a little studying up at home. There's a book I have, that I've had for years, since I was a teenager, that I always kept hidden from your mother. It's been invaluable to me over the years."

"What book? What's the title?" Steven asked.

"I didn't think you were interested in such things," Roy said. "I'm sure it'd all be a bunch of gobbledygook to you, or you'd just pick at it, 'cause that's what you do. So just trust me for now."

Steven wanted to object, but he knew Roy was right. He *would* pick at it, trying to discredit it. Probably not the "energy" Roy wanted right now.

"So you learned what we should do from this book?" Steven asked instead.

"Well, it gave me an idea," Roy replied, "to turn the tables, so to speak. So far, this has all been a one-way communication, it trying to talk to you. Or to scare you. But always initiated by it. This time *we're* going to initiate things. That sends a different signal. We'll see what happens."

"So you're not sure what's going to happen?"

"No, not really," Roy replied.

"So, we're just stirring things up then? Stirring the shit? That seems like a bad idea to me."

"This isn't my first time at the rodeo, kid," Roy said. "Give me a little bit of credit."

"What are you going to do, exactly?"

"A trance. It's like jumping in the river. But I'm in charge this time, I'm controlling the process. If I'm lucky we'll get some answers."

"What, like a séance?" Steven asked.

"Well, kind of, but you won't be participating," Roy answered. "We won't be holding hands around a table. But I will go into a trance, and come back out. I need you to keep an eye on me, make sure I don't trip over a rug or walk into a knife, that kind of thing."

"Has that ever happened? When you've done it before?" Steven asked.

"When you're in a trance," Roy said, "anything can happen. I might lose track of what I'm doing, physically. That's your job, to keep me safe. I'm trusting you."

Steven swallowed hard and pulled into the driveway of his house.

◊

Roy had placed a kitchen chair in the middle of the hallway where they had both seen the shadow the night before. He sat on the chair and handed Steven a scrap of cloth.

"Blindfold me," Roy said.

"What, you're starting it now? You're doing the trance now?"

"Yes," Roy replied. "I like the blindfold, it helps me concentrate. Another reason I need you to watch me."

"Wouldn't it be better…more successful if we waited until 3 a.m.? The time the knockings have been happening?"

"No," Roy answered. "It won't make any difference and it might make it worse. Three a.m. is *their* schedule. This is on *my* schedule. Now is fine. They're here, I know it."

Steven walked behind Roy and wrapped the light cloth around Roy's eyes. It wasn't thick enough to block much light, but would be enough to cause Roy to keep his eyes closed, which Steven guessed was its purpose.

"What do I do?" Steven asked, behind him.

"Come stand in front of me, but down the hall by the bedrooms. Keep an eye on me. You have the flashlight?"

"Yes," Steven replied.

"Good. I know you've never seen this before, but you've got to trust me. I might make all kinds of noises, but don't try to stop the trance until I take the blindfold off myself, OK? Promise me."

"I promise," Steven said, now more concerned than intrigued. Given what had happened to Roy the night before, he felt this was not going to end well.

"Good," Roy said. "Now, turn out the light and just stay quiet. Don't talk to me. It may take a while. We'll wait and let things play out."

◊

Steven had initially crouched down on his legs at the end of the hall but after ten minutes in the position he felt his legs beginning to cramp, and he shifted as quietly as he could into a cross-legged position. His father was still motionless in the chair halfway down the hall, and he couldn't hear any sound coming from him, not even breathing. Steven suppressed a sudden wave of panic at the idea of his father having a heart attack or a stroke while sitting there. *If he's had either,* Steven thought, *he'd be slumped over. But he's not – his head is upright, just as I left him ten minutes ago. Be patient.*

Another ten minutes passed, with Steven's mind racing. What would he do if the shadow appeared again? Would it start at the end of the hall? That would be behind Roy's head, would he know it was there? Steven strained to see the place where the shadow had first appeared. It looked normal.

Steven checked his watch. Another ten minutes passed, it had been thirty minutes. How long would this last? Would his father sit there until the knockings started at 3 a.m.? Steven felt his eyelids get heavy and he fought back the desire to shut them. His breathing was relaxed now, and the darkness and stillness seemed to envelop him the way the promise of pleasurable sleep washes over you just before it takes you. He felt his head nod, and he remembered thinking that letting it hang was a bad idea.

He thought he had nodded off for maybe a minute, but when he came back to awareness he was afraid it might have been longer. Things had changed in the hallway. The light was considerably less than before he had fallen asleep, and Steven had difficulty seeing his father distinctly; only his outline was visible from where he was sitting. His arms were suspended out to his sides, palms down, hanging as if they'd been raised by a puppeteer. He was breathing heavily with a raspy, grating breath as though he had just finished a marathon. With every exhale something vocal came out, but it was a short, guttural rumbling of his vocal chords, not a word or anything intelligible.

Steven remembered Roy's instruction to not talk to him or disturb the trance. But something was wrong, he felt it. There was a heaviness to the air in the hallway, it was thicker and more dense. He stood, and it felt like trying to stand from the bottom of a swimming pool. He felt a need to check on his father, to ensure he was OK. *I can at least get closer, watch him breathing,* he thought. *I won't interrupt him.*

Taking a step was like trying to move through sand. Steven was so jarred by the sensation he looked down at his lifted leg, trying to mentally will it to move. It was moving, but incredibly slowly. He felt exhausted at the effort it had taken to move a single step.

Roy continued to wheeze and grunt while Steven approached. His arms were outstretched to the sides, within inches of the hallway's walls, his fingers hanging. His head was thrown back, and Steven could see his Adam's apple rise and fall as the sounds emerged from his throat. He looked down, checking his father's body. To his horror he found the chair missing. His father was suspended, floating in the hallway.

Still, he did not say anything or attempt to touch him, to awaken him. Maybe it was the kid in him, but he felt he'd be in more trouble for violating his father's instructions than for letting this scene play out.

Looking up from the space below his father, he noticed something on the front of Roy's shirt. It was dark, and looked as though it had been dripped upon him. Roy slowly raised his head back into a normal position and Steven could see dark stains behind the blindfold, where his eyes would be. It was too dark to identify as blood for sure, but Steven didn't need the confirmation. He'd had enough. He was going to find out what had happened to his father, regardless of the trance. He moved his arm to reach for the blindfold, but found it to be moving at the glacial pace of his legs.

As his fingers reached it and began to pull it down from his father's forehead, he called out to him, but nothing came out. He felt his lips move, but no sound emerged. He felt the cold, dense air move into his mouth and lungs, blocking him. As the blindfold began to fall he could see his father's eyes – they had been gouged out, and were bleeding down his face and onto his shirt.

All at once, Steven felt the force of the air he had just inhaled move him. It rapidly pushed him, standing, back down the hallway he had just traversed. Steven flailed his arms to the side, trying to grab onto something to stop the movement, but couldn't reach anything, and he suspected that even if he had, he wouldn't have been able to stop himself – the force pushing him back was far too powerful. He felt his back hit the doorframe to his bedroom and he felt himself being forced back into his bed, face up. He had never felt anything like this before. It felt as though he was being assaulted, forced against his will, and he strained to raise his head or arms from the bed but could not. Something incredibly heavy was pressing down on him, on all parts of him, keeping him from moving. He had never felt *stopped* before. He felt violated and humiliated. In frustration he felt a tear escape his right eye and drip down his face to his ear and the pillow below. God knows what was happening to his father out in the hallway, but if it was anything like this, he was doomed.

The air darkened around him and he could no longer make out anything in his room. He felt consciousness leave him, and his last thoughts were: breathe. Breathe.

◊

Knock. Steven's eyes flew open he tried to turn his head toward the nightstand. It moved easily and he saw that it was 3 a.m. Another knock, the normal pattern. The horror of being unable to move in his own bed washed over him, and for a moment he was afraid he might not be able to sit up. But his brain gave the commands to his muscles and he found himself able to sit easily.

Another knock. *Dad!*

He raced into the hallway. It was empty. Grief and guilt hit him like a tidal wave. He was supposed to have kept an eye on him, to have protected him. But he had fallen asleep, or been forced asleep — he wasn't sure which — and now his father was missing. He called out for him, and began frantically searching the house. The final knock sounded. Steven raced from room to room, calling for Roy, checking corners, closets. Nothing upstairs. He went downstairs, continuing the search.

He found him in the bathroom downstairs. Roy was curled up in the bathtub, sleeping. Steven inspected him – no blood.

"Dad! Dad!" he shouted, attempting to wake him. "Please wake up, dad! You've got to wake up!"

He felt his father's body come to life and saw his eyes open to look at him. They were perfectly fine. Steven let out a sigh of relief, and sat back on the bathroom floor as his father awoke and gathered his wits.

"What time is it?" Roy asked.

"I have no idea," Steven replied, "but I'm so glad you're OK. Do you know what happened? Do you know how you got down here?"

Roy grabbed Steven's arm, pulled him. "Steven, I know exactly what happened. Take me home."

"What happened? Tell me," Steven implored.

"Not while we're still in the house. Take me to the car, drive me home."

They walked together, Steven offering to help Roy, but Roy insisting he didn't need help. Steven left Roy at the basement door while he went upstairs to get the car keys. When he returned they went to the car together. The chair that Roy had been sitting on in the hallway was on top of the hood.

"What the fuck?" Steven exclaimed.

"It's a message," Roy said. "Take it off and get in the car. We need to leave."

Seven

Back at Roy's house it was still dark, but Steven and Roy had turned on all the lights. Coffee was brewing in the kitchen, and Steven was trying to understand what had happened to Roy during the trance.

"So you know about the blood?" Steven asked. "Your eyes were gouged out."

"I saw it all. And more. Before you woke up in the hallway and tried to save me, I saw plenty. The faces you described in your bedroom, the disembodied head, all of it."

"They all appeared to you in the hallway?" Steven asked.

"No, not in the hallway. In the trance. It's a different place altogether. It felt like other trances I've been in, years ago. Something yearning, trying to communicate, and doing a damn poor job of it. But then, something else entirely different. Something else I've never felt before. Completely overwhelmed the trance, I lost all control of it. Then I felt my eyes being torn out. From then on, the whole thing felt like an assault."

Steven didn't know if he should share with his dad that he had had the same feeling during the incident. The feeling of being violated, assaulted. Having something overwhelm, control, and take something from you.

Roy paused, reflecting. "The only word for the latter part of the trance was evil. I know you don't think much of that, and to be honest with you that's not how I view things either. But this was dark, unusually dark. So opposite of anything I consider good and decent, the best word to describe it is evil."

Steven thought it best to let his father's assessment stand, but he didn't want to acknowledge that he'd had the same opinion. "Are you all right? Physically? It was horrifying to see you with your eyes torn out."

"I'm fine. Exhausted though. Feel like I need a week's sleep. I'll sleep today, and we'll try again tonight."

"What?"

"We'll do it again tonight," Roy said. "I need to go deeper."

"Like hell! You just said this – whatever it is – is evil. If that's true, shouldn't we steer clear?"

"Evil is only powerful if you don't stand up to it," Roy said.

"I *felt* that last night," Steven said. "It was powerful. It could just have easily killed me as held me down. Seems to me we're flirting with disaster here."

"It's not going to kill either of us," Roy replied.

"How do you know that?"

"It needs us alive. There's something it wants. Killing us doesn't achieve its goals. Listen, I'm a little more skilled in this than you're giving me credit for."

"Isn't some caution in order? I don't like the idea of you walking in there and just opening yourself up to it. It scares the hell out of me."

"Listen," Roy said. "What we need right now are answers. We've got a dozen pieces of a five hundred piece jigsaw puzzle, and the only way to get more is to dive in and get them. Besides, it'll drive me crazy not knowing. There's a few things I can do for precaution's sake. But we need answers Stevie, or you'll never have a night's sleep in that house again."

Steven felt his father winning the argument, but he still needed to take some action on his own. If more answers were needed, he knew where to get them. And this time he'd watch his rudeness to make sure the answers flowed.

Eight

Steven parked the Accord at trailer number 48 and waited for the truck at number 56 to pull away. It was 6:50, and if he had calculated correctly, John would leave for work in a few minutes. Then he'd walk over to Debra's trailer and start again. This time he'd make sure she knew he respected her beliefs.

He thought over the events of the last couple of days since he'd visited her last. The knockings that had, back then, terrorized him enough to seek her out now seemed like child's play, almost cute in comparison to the encounters he and his father had endured. While he was still a long way from being able to profess a belief in anything like religion or god, his experiences of the last 48 hours made it much easier to not crack a patronizing smile when someone said "evil."

Steven saw the truck back out of their driveway and head the other direction. *There must be a closer exit that way,* Steven thought, noting to try it himself when he left.

He waited a few minutes, not really sure why. If John was going to return home, it could happen any time he was there, not just in the first few minutes. But he waited nonetheless, thinking it might lower the chances.

When he felt it was safe he walked up to the trailer and knocked on the door. After a moment it opened.

"Oh. It's you," Debra said, surprised.

"Yeah, it's me. I was wondering if we could try again. With me keeping my mouth shut this time," he smiled.

She smiled back, thought about it. "Sure. John just left. But I suppose you knew that. Come on in."

Steven stepped up into the trailer and resumed his seat on the cluttered couch. Not much had changed since he left two days ago, including the cat piss. He resigned to not let it show on his face.

Debra sat down across from him. "I gotta tell you, you look awful. I don't mean it personal, but obviously things aren't getting better."

"You're right," Steven answered. "They're not. I had a few more experiences in the house and decided to get my dad involved. He's had some experience with events like these."

"Oh, has he?" Debra asked. "Did he see something in the house?"

"Yes, he did." Steven was unsure how far he should go, but he did want Debra to feel comfortable with him, enough to speak to him about her father-in-law's experience. "He went into a sort of trance, and we both saw a figure, kind of a shadow, that had — "

Debra raised a hand, cutting him off. "Don't, don't tell me," she shuddered. "It'll just give me nightmares. I try to keep my mind clear of those kind of things. Just the times I felt it when I visited Ben were enough for me. Sounds like you got a good dose of it yourself."

"That's a good way to put it," Steven said. "Listen," he continued, "the last time I was here, I really don't think I was ready to hear what you had to say. My apologies. After what I've seen and been through since then, trust me, I'm ready. It's just that, my father and I, we're struggling for answers. I can't afford to just move and abandon the place. He's dead set on continuing his trances in the house, to try and figure it out. I'm not sure there's anything to figure out, it might just be unsolvable and I'll be forced to live with it or take a financial loss. But I did think, after remembering our conversation from Monday, that I had stupidly cut you off before you could tell me something important. Something about your father-in-law. I might be grasping at straws here, but I'm hoping you can share some more with me, something that might help us figure things out."

Debra lit a cigarette, took a long drag on it.

"Anything," Steven continued, "anything that might help, even if it seems irrelevant."

"The only thing we didn't talk about when you were here before," Debra said, "was Ben's decline. The problems at that house developed over time, they weren't the way they are now, when Ben first moved there. Things all went downhill for him after Little Tony disappeared. Little Tony was Ben's youngest son. They called him Little Tony because Ben had a brother named Anthony that Little Tony was named after. Anyway, he was six years old when he went missing. Ben always let him play in the yard with neighbor kids, and always he'd come in for dinner, just like the neighbor kids. This one day, he didn't come in."

Steven leaned back in the couch, afraid of knocking something over, but needing to adjust. "He disappeared?" he asked.

"Literally without a trace," she replied. "Of course Ben talked to every single neighbor, and all the kids, asking them if they'd seen Little Tony that day. No one had, or if they had, they didn't say anything. Ben put up posters all over the neighborhood. Cops were involved, but after a while, with no leads, and after deciding that Ben wasn't the cause, the cops just dropped it. Another missing child case. Apparently it happens a lot."

Steven listened intently. The information was like manna to him, giving him new options he desperately needed.

"Ben spent all of his time searching," Debra continued. "He was constantly in his car, for weeks, driving up and down streets. He bought maps of the city and was methodically searching through parks and fields. Sometimes people would help him, we did many times, but most of the time he did it himself. Then one day he stopped. We thought he'd given up, exhausted from all the hunting. But instead of looking, he became paranoid. He'd invent all kinds of crazy theories about what had happened to Little Tony and he'd try to convince me and John of them. We weren't having it, but we weren't going to tell Ben he was crazy, either. I think John half believed some of his ideas 'cause John was a wreck too. There was a big age difference between John and Little Tony, but they loved each other and John spent a lot of time with him. John was just as devastated as Ben. I figured the best thing was to let them both work through it in their own way. John eventually came out of it, but things never improved for Ben. He seemed to become more and more obsessed with theories."

Debra pulled out another cigarette, chain-lighting it from the first. "At one point we thought he had made a turn, that maybe he was recovering from the grief and starting to return to some kind of normal life, because he seemed better, not always talking about Little Tony and the theories. He actually seemed at peace. I remember John and I talking about how maybe things would get back to some kind of normal routine, as normal as they can get when you've had such a major loss. But it didn't last long. Something hit him physically. I think it was all the stress that had built up during the whole thing, just took its toll on his body. He went from being perfectly fine and able to get around, to being unable to get out of bed, in a matter of weeks. That's when we would visit him, try to keep him company, keep his spirits up. We went over many times. But it got so I couldn't set foot in that damned house – it was just so oppressive. Towards the end I couldn't stand to breathe the air, I didn't want it in me. I know how strange that must sound."

"I've had the same feeling," Steven assured her. "I know what you mean."

"So I don't know if that helps. That's what happened to Ben. He developed those crazy ideas, but in my heart I know he wasn't crazy, just grief stricken. People do strange things when they're in that much despair. But that wasn't what killed him. Something else killed him. That house."

"Killed him?" Steven asked.

"That's right. Killed him. There was something there he just couldn't see anymore, couldn't stand to look at. That's why he cut out his eyes. He wasn't crazy. He was driven to that. I got a taste of it whenever I was there. You know what I'm talking about."

"Yes, I think I do," Steven replied.

Nine

Steven arrived back late at his father's house, thinking they would pack up and head back over to his house for the second trance. But upon arriving at Roy's house, Steven could tell it wasn't going to happen.

"I'm exhausted, there's no way," Roy said. "I think I just need to get a good night's sleep and we'll tackle it tomorrow night. But I insist that you sleep here tonight, Stevie. You shouldn't go back into that house. At least not alone. Here you'll be safe, and we'll both be able to recharge our batteries. Tomorrow we can come back at it, stronger."

This made sense to Steven and he agreed. He was concerned about his father's health already, and felt going back to the house tonight for another dose of what happened the night before was pushing it. If the ghosts had been there for fifteen years they would last for another night.

Steven found himself in the room he grew up in, a room his mother had turned into a guest room years ago. But Steven still remembered the bunk bed he shared with Bernie, the walls that held posters, and the closet that had given them both nightmares. *Funny how the things that scare us are so universal,* he thought.

The last time Steven had stayed in the guest room had been the days between his mother's passing and the funeral. Those had been strange days. In some ways, Claire's passing had been a relief, but viewing it as such immediately brought guilt. Both his and Bernie's relationship with their mother had been strained at best. She was always the disciplinarian; Roy never got the chance to fill that role. When both Steven and Bernie left for college and stopped attending church, she was like a harpy, forever trying to get them to repent and go. They tried to handle her gently, hoping she'd eventually accept the fact that neither of them had any interest in religion or following her advice in that regard. When she didn't get the message, it became easier to just distance themselves from her. Bernie used geography and Steven used work: Bernie moved to San Antonio, and Steven was too busy to be around, no time for the Jesus lectures. They rarely visited.

Of course, this came at a price. They were both distant from Roy, too. Steven realized he'd learned more about Roy in the past few days than he knew from his entire life before. He wondered what Bernie would think of this whole thing.

Steven closed his eyes and let sleep come. If he could even get half of a night straight through, he'd take it.

◊

It was the kind of nightmare you tried to force yourself out of. In a pool of water, daylight receding. Falling, trying to hold your breath, but eventually having to let it in, water rushing into your lungs. Light beginning to condense. He knew it was a dream while it was happening, and he willed himself to wake up. As he opened his eyes, the ceiling above him was unfamiliar, but he oriented himself within moments. His mouth felt dry; he'd been drooling on the pillow, and it was soaked. He flipped it over, but now he was waking up. *So much for sleeping straight through,* he thought. He decided to make his way to the kitchen for some water. The layout of the house came back to him quickly. He glanced at the door to his father's room – it was closed. He made his way to the kitchen, found a glass, filled it, and downed it. Sat it down quietly. He walked back to the guest room, hoping to fall asleep quickly, when he noticed the door to Roy's room was now ajar.

The same dread and heavy air filled the hallway as he made his way down to his father's room. He pushed the door open.

In a way, it didn't surprise him. He'd taken Roy's opinion that they were safe here at face value. But as soon as he saw it, he knew it had been a bad assumption. In the middle of the room stood the shadow, its eyes gleaming, focused intently on Roy. Like before, Roy was rigid and shaking. This time Steven didn't try to rouse Roy – he already knew what it was doing to him. He approached the shadow, raising his voice. "Goddamn it, leave him alone!" he shouted.

As he neared the shadow he had a sensation of a cold, icy knife slicing through his skin. The pain was incredible, and he jumped back. In his peripheral vision he saw Roy soften and still, and he knew the shadow had released him. Its eyes turned to center on Steven. He stared it down, neither of them moving. He noticed Roy waking, taking in the scene in the middle of the room. Roy arose and approached the shadow too. Steven felt he should not lose eye contact with the shadow – as long as he didn't, he felt the shadow didn't know about Roy's movement, it remained focused on him. Steven was expecting an attack, for it to turn on him the way it had on Roy, but it didn't move, it didn't seem to want anything of him. It was just watching him. He noticed Roy behind it. Roy was lowering his head, as though he was praying. *Going into a trance?* Steven thought. The eyes in the shadow slowly closed, and the ambient light in the room began to appear inside it. Within moments, it was gone. Roy raised his head.

"So much for being safe here," Steven said.

"Yeah," Roy replied. "I think I have really misjudged this thing." He was rubbing his arms, obviously in pain once again.

"How did you make it go away?" Steven asked.

"I willed it. It was easy," Roy said. "You could try the next time you see it."

"I don't think it would work," Steven said.

"It might," Roy said. "You just close your eyes, concentrate, and mentally say, 'go away.'"

"Really? That's all?" Steven asked.

"Yes," replied Roy, "and you have the advantage of being awake when this thing is attacking me. I'm asleep, I can't do it. It knows that."

"Is that what it's doing?" Steven asked. "Attacking you?"

"You felt it last night. What did it feel like to you?"

"Yes, I would call it an attack. It felt like I was being raped. Not physically, but mentally. It was taking something from me."

"Next time defend yourself," Roy replied. "You might be surprised at what you're able to do."

"Do you think it will come back?" Steven asked.

"Why not?" Roy replied. "I was wrong about it not following us here. For whatever reason it wants us, it'll just wait until we're asleep and attack again."

"Then we can sleep in shifts," Steven said.

"Good idea. You sleep first," Roy said. "I'm coming at this the wrong way, and I need to study up before we approach it tonight at the house, discover what I'm doing wrong."

"With your secret book?" Steven asked.

"Yes," Roy replied, "with my secret book that might save your ass. Try to sleep as much as you can. I'll wake you in a few hours, and we'll trade off."

Ten

Steven sat cross-legged at the end of the hallway, once again waiting for something to happen. Roy was seated in the hallway, blindfold on, waiting as well. Steven hoped things might play out more benignly tonight, but either way, he was determined to get more answers.

He and Roy had traded off the night before, keeping an eye on each other while the other slept. Whether their approach worked or they just got lucky, nothing appeared and no attacks occurred. They both had received much needed sleep, and they slept into the late morning, anticipating another late night at Steven's with the second trance.

Roy had spent a good amount of the day with his book. He complained multiple times to Steven of being "rusty" and that if he'd been more in practice, certain things wouldn't have gone past him. Steven wasn't entirely sure what he was referring to, other than the idea that the shadow couldn't follow them to Roy's, which was obviously wrong. But for the most part Roy seemed confident he knew what he was getting into with the second trance, and he talked as much about being prepared with defenses as he did getting answers to their questions. It was clear to Steven that Roy was afraid of the shadow, of what it might do to either of them if they weren't prepared to deal with it.

The hallway sat still. It had been half an hour, the same amount of time they waited two nights ago before things went to hell. Steven had fallen asleep then, and he felt that he had let his father down. But Roy had asked him details about that, and had assured him he hadn't fallen asleep on his own, that he had been "led to sleep" by the forces in the house. It made Steven feel marginally better, but he still resolved to stay awake tonight. Twice he had interrupted the shadow attacking his father, and he didn't want to find out what might happen to Roy if there was another attack, or, god forbid, an attack that he didn't interrupt.

The heaviness was returning, and it made Steven think of how Debra had described it. It seemed as though the air became thicker, and there was additional pressure in the house. This was the same as two nights ago – just before he fell asleep, the same feeling. *If I don't fall asleep, or if it doesn't think I'm asleep, it won't appear,* Steven thought. *Sleep is part of this. I need to fake it. I need it to think I'm asleep.* He closed his eyes, and let his mind wander, but kept pinching his left hand with his right. He had no idea if this would work, but he stuck with it for several minutes.

Just as he thought he might have to change technique, Steven heard Roy speaking, but it didn't sound like Roy. "Come to me...come to me..." At first he thought Roy was speaking to him, that he should get up and walk over to him. But he repeated the phrase over and over, dozens of times. It began to take on the quality of a chant. Steven knew he was not speaking to him.

Steven saw, over Roy's head, a face appear. It was one of the child faces he'd encountered in his bedroom the first night. It was floating, hovering above Roy. Steven's legs tensed as he felt an instinctive need to protect his father. But the more he looked at the face, the more he registered sadness and pain rather than evil intent, and Steven calmed with the realization that the face was not a threat to Roy. The face seemed lost, and Roy's calls, or whoever's voice was coming from Roy, were beckoning the child. And now, where it had looked like one face, there appeared to be several, all overlaying each other.

Steven felt a wave of pressure pass over him and the hallway seemed much darker. Roy's voice seemed muddled, like it was coming through a tube. Steven looked at his arm and knew if he tried to raise it, it would move slowly, as it had the other night. The thickness had arrived. He pushed an image of himself sleeping to his forethoughts, and let the images and sounds of the hallway recede.

In a matter of seconds, the hallway had filled with water. Steven, still sitting cross-legged at the end of the hall, was immersed up to his waist. *I'm hallucinating*, he thought. *No, you're not hallucinating. You're seeing what Roy is seeing. You've jumped in.*

Once again Roy's arms were extended to his sides. The darkness in the hallway made Roy only a silhouette. "It's over now…it's over now…" Roy was saying. The faces had disappeared, but something else was building. The feeling of sadness and loss was now replaced by dread.

As Steven watched, a figure rose from the water, next to Roy. It was shaped like a man, but it was twisted and grotesque, as though something had genetically gone wrong. Parts of it appeared more animal than human, but even the animal parts were wrong. Steven strained his eyes to take it in, to make a mental picture of this creature. Once it had fully emerged, it turned to Roy. Steven studied its face, but the bends and folds of skin where skin shouldn't be made it hard for him to process what he was seeing. Its eyelids were closed. It had no hair, and the bare skin looked armored in places, like a reptile or a beetle. Flaps of skin hung down from the forehead and cheeks, as though it was inside a flesh costume that was too big for it. Its chest was massive and its torso was shaped like a man's, tapering at the waist. Its phallus was definitely not human, it looked more like a dog's. Its legs disappeared into the water. As Steven watched, it took a step toward Roy. Then it opened its eyes, and Steven recognized them immediately.

He knew he needed to send it way, as he had the first night. He attempted to stand, but his motions were slowed by the resistance of the water and the air in the room – he was moving through clear quicksand again, just like before. It took an eternity just to make a step.

As he progressed towards Roy and the figure he saw its lips move. He couldn't tell what it was saying, but he could hear Roy's replies.

"It doesn't matter…it doesn't matter," Roy was repeating. Was he attempting to repel the figure? Or was he speaking to him, Steven? He lifted another foot and with agonizing slowness continued his march toward the couple, engaged in a conversation he could only half make out.

"Why should I care? The only thing that matters is gone," he heard Roy speak. It was Roy's voice, but it wasn't Roy speaking. The figure was having a conversation with someone other than Roy.

The figure reached a hand towards Roy, and Steven saw Roy's body go rigid. *The attack has begun, I've got to do something,* Steven thought. He focused his mind and shouted

"BE GONE" as loudly as he could. Nothing seemed to come out. He was too far away. He focused all of his energy on moving closer, taking as many steps as he could, as quickly as he could. Roy was shaking now, and a panic set in Steven, feeling that if he didn't do something soon, Roy wouldn't last. He was a step closer to them and he tried again: "BE GONE. LEAVE HIM ALONE."

It worked, or at least for a moment he thought it had worked. The figure's eyes shifted from Roy to him. At the same moment its eyes reached him, Steven felt all of the water in front of him rush towards him, an additional force pushing him back. It pushed him off his feet, and he fell backwards into the water.

It was just like the dream. Everything in slow motion, holding your breath, but knowing you were going to have to open your lungs eventually and then you'd be in trouble. He moved his arms to push himself up from the floor. It took forever. The water was rushing at him with the force of a fast moving river. It took all of his strength to fight against it, get his arm into position against the floor, and push himself up above the water level. As his head cleared the water, he gasped for air, sucking in a huge lungful, and raising his knee to stand.

How long have I been underwater? he wondered. As he looked up, the scene had changed. Roy was pinned against the hallway wall opposite the figure. There was a knife in his hand, and as Steven cleared the water from his eyes, he saw that Roy's throat was cut. It was a ragged, gaping wound, and blood was pouring from it down his shirt and into the water below. Roy's body was still shaking, and the sight aroused such anger in Steven that he focused his mind with all of the energy he had left and shouted, "LET HIM GO!"

In the blink of an eye the water was gone and the ability to breathe normally returned. Roy's body slipped from the wall into a crumpled heap on the hallway floor. The eyes in the shadow closed, and Steven saw it descend into the floor. Steven rushed over to his father, checking him for damage. There was none, no blood, no cut throat. As Roy came to, Steven asked him if he was ok.

"Hurts. All over."

"You were up on the wall," Steven said. "When it ended, you slid down to the floor."

"Did you see it all?" Roy asked. "Did you see *it*?"

"Yes," Steven replied. "I didn't fall asleep. I saw the whole thing. I saw it."

Steven raised Roy to his feet, and they walked out of the hallway and into the kitchen. They both sat down in kitchen chairs and stared at each other.

"Do you need some aspirin?" Steven asked.

"I'm thinking whiskey," Roy replied.

"I've got whiskey," Steven said, and went to the liquor cabinet. He brought back a bottle and two glasses, and they each poured a shot and downed it in silence.

After a while Steven said, "I'm not sure I can do this kind of thing again. You were suspended on the wall with your throat cut. I could barely move to do anything about it."

"But you did do something about it," Roy said. "You ended it. And we got what we were looking for. Well, part of it, anyway."

"What part? What did you learn for all that?" Steven asked.

"For starters, I figured out we've been looking at this all wrong."

"What do you mean?"

"There are different entities here," Roy explained. "We thought we were dealing with the ghost of the man who committed suicide, but it's much deeper than that."

"How many entities?"

"Well, there's two for sure. Probably more. Ben is one. He's the one I'm most able to contact. Many of the manifestations we've seen have come from him. The knocking, for example, that's Ben. But whenever I make contact with Ben, a second entity shows up. Every time."

"The shadow?" Steven asked.

"Yes, but you saw him tonight, didn't you? The real thing, not just the shadow with eyes."

"Yes, I saw him," Steven said. The image of the distorted and twisted shape was still vivid in his mind.

"I believe," said Roy, "that that thing, the shadow, is the reason Ben took out his eyes. When I was in the trance, I was able to see things from Ben's perspective. He was saddled with an enormous amount of grief. I remembered that feeling when Claire passed, it feels like a mountain weighing you down, and that you'll never get over it. And he was being haunted – attacked, really – by this thing, this shadow. It had been attacking him for a while. And I could tell Ben knew the shadow, he knew who or what it was. Ben's despair was so large, once he realized that the shadow would never stop, would never go away, he couldn't bear to see it anymore, it horrified and sickened him, and he got to a point where he just wanted it to stop. In the trance I felt what he felt when he decided to remove his eyes. I understood it completely."

Steven gulped. He wasn't sure what kind of depths a person had to sink to to take that kind of a step, and the thought of it unnerved him. It made him feel a little sick to his stomach.

"It didn't work," Roy continued. "He didn't have to see it anymore, but it didn't stop the shadow from attacking. He was having the life drained from him every night, every time he slept. Not being able to see the shadow made it easier to endure the rest of what he went through."

"So he killed himself to end the pain?" Steven asked.

"Did it in that bathtub," Roy replied. "But he was also trying to stop it, the shadow. He was denying it something by killing himself; his suicide was also an attack back at it, his way of striking back."

"I can't say I understand that," Steven said.

"It's because it wasn't just haunting him, it was using him, draining him," Roy said. "He wanted to deny it any more of himself."

"But why? Why was it after him?" Steven asked.

"That's something we don't know yet," Roy said. "But there's another thing I learned that might answer that question."

"What is that?"

"There's something in the hallway that we need to find. Something Ben hid."

◊

Steven used a screwdriver to pry the baseboard away from the wall in the area that Roy suggested they try first. It exposed the corner where the floorboards met the wall.

"Look along the edge," Roy said. "See if one of the floorboards is a fraction of an inch shorter, or doesn't go all the way to the wall."

Steven shined a flashlight into the corner of the wall and floor, on his hands and knees, inspecting each floorboard. They all came flush against the wall, no spaces, nothing unusual. "Nothing," he said.

"Try over here," Roy said, prying the baseboard off the opposite wall himself.

Steven ran the flashlight into the corner again, looking for the board Roy described. He found one near the middle of the hallway. "Here!" he said, and began to pry it using the screwdriver. It popped up with a little effort, along with a couple of attached pieces of the hardwood floor. There was nothing directly underneath it, but shining the flashlight into the hole Steven could see that there was a space that bent to the left. Steven turned to Roy. "Ben showed you this?"

"Yes," Roy replied. "in a way. He felt it was part of the solution, and part of the problem."

"What did he mean by that?" Steven asked, suddenly not sure he wanted to find what lay below.

"No idea," said Roy. "But we need it if we're going to figure this out."

Steven sat thinking. He wasn't at all sure he wanted to reach his hand into the space and search for whatever might be lurking there.

"Oh for fuck's sake," Roy said. "Get out of the way, I'll do it."

◊

"This is all just crazy lunatic rambling," Steven said as he flipped through the book they had found under the hallway floorboards. "Debra mentioned this to me. Ben went off his rocker, completely paranoid. This reads like a stream of consciousness from a sick mind."

"Ben might have been paranoid," Roy said, "but he had every right to be. And he wasn't unbalanced, I'm sure of that."

"Then you'll have to explain this to me," Steven said, abandoning it, tossing it to his father on the other side of the kitchen table. "It seems like the crazy shit you see on the walls in a serial killer's lair in a movie. It's useless."

Roy took the book and began reading through it. "Yeah, I see what you mean," he sighed, turning the pages. "I can't think straight right now anyway. Let's get some shuteye and approach this fresh in the morning." Roy closed the book and stood, but his legs gave out under him, and he fell to the floor.

"Damn it, goddamn it," Roy exclaimed. Steven rushed over and grabbed Roy's arm, attempting to lift him. "What happened?"

"I'm fine, I'm fine," Roy said, attempting to get to his feet. "I just need to…" and he slumped into Steven's arms.

"Dad? Can you hear me?" Steven asked, carrying his father back to the kitchen chair and setting him into it as carefully as he could. Roy fell forward onto the kitchen table and stayed there. Steven checked Roy's breathing and heartbeat, both of which seemed fine. Maybe Roy was just exhausted and needed rest, but he wasn't taking chances. With everything he had seen his father go through the past few days he was surprised it hadn't happened earlier. Roy was a tough old man, but he *was* old, and he had his limits.

As much as Roy would be against it, Steven picked up the phone and dialed 911.

Eleven

"Here, I brought you something," Steven said, tossing Ben's book from the floorboards into Roy's lap on the hospital bed.

"Unhook me and take me home, goddamnit," Roy said.

"Not a chance. Not until they tell me you're OK," Steven said.

"I'm telling you I'm perfectly fine. They wouldn't know anyway," Roy replied.

"Well, humor me. The doctor is supposed to come around in a few minutes. In the meantime," Steven said, pulling up a chair, "I wish to retract some of what I said about this book last night."

"What was that?" Roy asked.

"Turns out there is something useful in it. After I left here last night, I went home and tried to sleep, but couldn't. So I started going through it, more carefully, page by page. These pages in the middle, the ones that look like scrapbooks, where he taped in newspaper articles?" Steven said, turning the book to the pages to show Roy, and pointing to one in particular. "That's what I found."

Roy took the book and read what Steven had pointed out. It was a *Seattle Times* article taped to the pages of the journal. *Suspect Released in Abduction Case,* the title read. "Hand me my glasses," Roy said, pointing to the stand by the bed. Steven grabbed them and handed them over to Roy, who put them on and began to read, sometimes muttering the words, other times stopping to shoot a glace up at Steven, who stood by the bed watching Roy's reaction.

Roy finished the article, and turned back a page. Here was another article, this one about cancer radiation from power lines. Before it was an article on contaminated baby food from China. "OK, what does it mean?" Roy asked. "I don't see any connection."

"That article on the abduction suspect is the Rosetta Stone to the rest of the book. Not the stuff that comes before it, but everything after. I've marked some other sections with post it notes. I want you to read them, but read them with the abduction article in mind. Everything before it is Ben trying to find an answer, rambling, lost. He found what he was looking for when he found that article."

Roy turned to the first bookmark Steven had inserted into the book, and read some of that page. The penmanship was very small. Ben had managed to cram thousands of words on a single page, filling every available space. The overall effect of the page was lunacy, but the content, read as Steven instructed, became more lucid with each word.

Roy stopped and flipped to the next bookmark. Same reaction. As Roy continued to work his way through the sections Steven had prepared, he watched the color drain from Roy's face. When he reached the last one, Roy glanced up at Steven and said, "You gotta get me outta here. I insist. Right now."

"Wait, there's more," said Steven, smiling, pleased that his father seemed to pick up on what he had discovered in the book.

"More?" asked Roy, clearly intrigued.

At that moment the doctor walked into the room, and Roy handed the book back to Steven. Steven guessed Roy preferring to not be discovered with something so lunatic by a doctor who would be giving him a prognosis.

They chatted for a few moments, with the doctor saying all tests were negative and giving Roy a clean bill of health. Steven asked about the cause of Roy's collapse.

"Well, Roy tells me he hasn't had a good night's sleep in several days," said the doctor. "I'd say it was due to exhaustion. Nothing else appears wrong. You can go, but I'm prescribing sleep – lots of it."

Roy sat upright in bed, looking between the doctor and Steven, with a grin on his face. "Great, let's go," Roy said. "Where's my clothes?"

The doctor held his hand up to stop Roy. "I'll need you to wait here until a nurse comes around and removes the IV. Then you'll find your clothes in the drawer of the cabinet by the door. But please don't leave the room until a nurse brings the paperwork by for you to sign." The doctor turned to Steven. "You'll make sure he gets out of here OK?"

"Yeah, I'm driving him home," said Steven.

"Great. If this should happen again in the next 72 hours bring him back in. Thank you both, have a nice day," the doctor said, and left the room.

"If this is right," Roy said as soon as the door had shut, "Ben found who killed his son."

"Little Tony," Steven offered, "and others. Who knows how many more."

"I'm going to guess four," Roy said.

Steven looked at him, knowing he was right. "Yeah, four."

They paused. Roy cleared his throat. "OK, let me start this again, see if we're thinking the same thing. Ben is searching for what happened to his son. He tried several wild ideas, but they're all just stabs in the dark. But then he settles on this abduction story, decided that this suspect they released was the man who abducted Little Tony. Then what?"

"He stalks the guy," Steven offered. "I know I would. Ben had all the time in the world on his hands, remember, he'd been combing through parks and fields and abandoned properties. He switches his focus to this guy, to see if his theory is correct."

"Because," Roy interjected, "if it is, he might be able to save Little Tony."

"So," Steven continued, "he stalks the guy, until something confirms to him that he's the guilty one. He discovers that Little Tony is gone, all the children are gone; this guy has killed them. In his anger, he kills the guy, and he disposes of the body. He feels a sense of justice, that he's avenged the death of his son, and he's taken a killer off the streets, saved countless others."

"But that's not the end of it."

"No, it's not. Because whatever he killed came back to haunt him. All of Ben's journal, following that article, is about the stalking and the haunting. He conveniently left the killing out."

"I would have left it in," Roy said with indignation. "Any father would have been justified. I'da helped him pull the trigger."

"I know," Steven acknowledged, "but this guy's no John Wayne and there's no happy ending. He kills the guy, he disposes of the body, it comes back to haunt him, and, in the end, it haunts him to death."

"That means," Roy said, "that Ben's reason for haunting you has been to alert you to this fellow. We've been thinking the haunting was because Ben killed himself in the house, but that's only part of it. The haunting is because Ben wants you to know who he killed, and why he killed him, because the job isn't finished – it's still alive, in some form, still preying on people."

"All of the occurrences I experienced, with the exception of the shadow, those came from Ben?" Steven asked.

"I believe so," Roy replied. "The shadow was a different matter altogether."

"But if the shadow was after Ben, and it succeeded in killing him by getting him to cut his own throat, why continue haunting the house? He's achieved his goal at that point, right?"

Roy thought about this. "It could be," he said, "that we stirred it back up."

A nurse appeared at the door, asking to remove the IV in Roy's arm, which he eagerly presented to her to facilitate the task. In another twenty minutes they were in Steven's car and headed back to Roy's house.

"What did you mean when you said we 'stirred it up'?" Steven asked.

"Before I came over that first night," Roy replied, "what you'd seen was limited to things Ben wanted you to see. All of the manifestations – the knocking, the faces, the head over the bathtub – that was all Ben, things that referenced him, his knowledge of events. I show up two nights later, and *bam!*" Roy clapped his hands together for dramatic effect, "the shadow appears, and has ever since. I think it was stirred up by me, by my involvement."

"By you? How?" Steven asked.

"I think my involvement was what both Ben and the shadow wanted all along. I think they used you to get me involved. The reason why the shadow attacks me, why it never even showed up until I arrived at your place, is because it needs, it eats, what I have. It attacks me and not you because I'm stronger, I've got the gift. And it sucks it out of me – that's what it's doing when it attacks, it's draining me. It's why you put me in the hospital."

"But why?" Steven asked. "I understand it attacking Ben, but why you? Because you're able to communicate to Ben?"

Roy sighed. "I don't know. Nothing's surfaced that explains why. I still need to figure that out. What is our next step?"

"No more trances," Steven said. "I mean it. If you're right, they only give the thing what it wants, more access to you."

"Fine," Roy shot back, "but I intend to go through Ben's journal with a fine tooth comb."

"I think that's a great idea, so long as you stay awake." Steven pulled into Roy's driveway, but left the car running.

"You're not coming in?" Roy asked.

"Nope. You get to work on that journal, see if anything pops out. I'm going to do some research on that news article and the abduction suspect."

"You be careful," Roy warned, getting out of the car. "We don't know everything we're dealing with here, so don't take risks."

"Look who's talking," Steven shot back, and put the car in reverse.

Twelve

Steven returned home from the library a little after 5 p.m. The house was trashed – the hallway was still torn up, the kitchen hadn't been dealt with in days. Steven ignored it all and called Roy.

"Get in your car and meet me at Bent's in ten minutes," Steven said.

"I'm not hungry," Roy replied. "Besides, I think I dug up something you should know."

"Well, I am hungry." He checked his watch. "Meet me there at quarter of six. And I have something for you, too."

"Fine, goddamn it..." Roy said, hanging up. Steven grabbed a couple of flashlights, then rummaged in a closet for a pair of binoculars that normally only came out for concerts. He stuffed them into a duffel bag and went back downstairs and out the basement door.

Within a few minutes he was at Bent's. Roy wasn't there yet, so he ordered and sat in a booth that seemed to offer the most privacy. He was three bites into his burger when Roy arrived and sat at the table.

"You having anything?" Steven asked.

"I told you I wasn't hungry," Roy replied.

"You gotta keep your strength up. You're an old man and I wouldn't want to have to put you back into the hospital just because you hadn't been eating."

"I'm not hungry because I already ate. And you need to show more respect for your elders."

Steven brushed it off. "You said you found something?"

"Yes, I have," said Roy. "The sections you marked in Ben's journal aren't the half of it. Yes, Ben hunted him down and yes, he was terrorized by the guy's ghost. But I think Ben must have talked to the guy at some point, confronted him, had some kind of conversation with him. He knows things about him, or claims to, and he uses some terms to describe him that I had to reference in my book."

"Your secret book? His name was Lukas Johansen, by the way," Steven added.

"Sounds like you made some progress, too," Roy said. "Well, for starters, Ben didn't think he was human. Not that he was inhuman because he killed people, I think Ben thought he was another species altogether. We saw what he really looks like the other night, in the trance. Definitely not human. Ben keeps referring to him as a pupa, something in development. What he was changing into was some kind of being that would live forever. Ben thought this guy was trying to become immortal."

"What, like a vampire?" Steven asked incredulously.

"No, not like that. Although there are some disturbing similarities as far as blood is concerned. Our friend Lukas was completing some kind of process or recipe that he needed. And here's the horrible part, and it probably made the guy very easy for Ben to kill: it called for the bodies of children."

Steven stopped chewing his hamburger and stared at Roy, unsure if he should swallow.

"I know," said Roy, "disgusting."

"Are you sure?" Steven mouthed around his food.

"No, I don't know any of this for sure, but Ben believed it. Ben had decided this Lukas guy had abducted his son, killed him, drained him of his blood, and ingested it. And that he had done it to others, and would continue to do it, until he achieved his goal."

"Immortality?" Steven asked.

"That's what Ben thought, it's what he's written here. But Ben cut the guy's plans short. Ben describes it as smashing the moth in the cocoon."

Steven considered this. "Sounds like he managed to eke out some immortality – he's still terrorizing people from the grave."

"This guy is like a battery running with a very low charge. He needs an occasional recharge to keep going, he can't do it on his own. When he finds someone like me, hell, I'm a fucking three course banquet to him."

"Can we put a stop to it?" Steven asked.

"Don't know," Roy said. "Ben killed him. I don't know how, but it obviously wasn't enough to end things. I'm not sure how you deal with something like this."

"Well, I know what we're going to do next," Steven said, finishing his burger. "Lukas Johansen used to live two blocks from here – a house on 34th."

"We're going to check it out?" Roy asked with some excitement.

"That's what I'm thinking." They left the booth and headed to Steven's car.

◊

"That's it straight ahead," Steven said, pointing to a house further down the block from where they were parked.

"How can you be sure, you can't see the numbers from here," Roy replied.

Steven pulled out his cell phone and showed Roy the house on Google. "You can see every house online. Street view."

"Well, that's amazing," Roy said.

"You'd know that if you'd get a computer," Steven said.

"I don't need every house in my phone," Roy said.

Steven dropped it. His father was never going to own a computer or a smartphone, and they both knew it.

"So, what are you thinking?" Roy asked. "Stake it out? See who comes and goes?"

Steven was using the binoculars, mindful of how he must look to any neighbors along the street who might be checking out the parked car in front of their houses. "Well," he said, "yeah, that's what I'm thinking. Of course, Lukas is dead, so we won't be seeing him. At least I don't think we will."

Steven scanned the front of the house. It was a turn of the century classic Victorian, but it was in need of repair and a new paint job. All of the curtains were closed except for one upstairs bedroom, and there were cracks in the glass of several of the windows. The trees and plants in front of the house were in need of pruning and weeds were abundant. The small lawn in front was a month from its last mowing. There was no garage, and from this angle they couldn't see anything in the backyard.

Over the course of the next hour, Steven and Roy watched as several kids came and went from the house. They were all in their early twenties and dressed in black from head to toe.

"I've never seen such a thing," said Roy.

"What?" asked Steven.

"All the black clothes. Is it a cult?"

"No, they're goth kids, Dad. It's a style. Although from the goth kids I knew, wearing black was almost like a religion to them."

"I don't get it," Roy answered. "It's dark enough here without running around completely in black. So they're just kids?"

"Yup," Steven answered.

"I'm gonna go talk to them," Roy said, opening the car door.

"Wait!" Steven cried, but Roy was already marching up the road. Steven jumped out and ran up to his dad.

"What are you doing?" he asked Roy.

"I'm going to talk to them," Roy said, walking briskly towards the house. "We're not learning anything just sitting in the car."

"I was thinking we'd watch the place from a distance, see who comes and goes, see if there's any threats we should know about, that kind of thing, before we storm in."

Roy was undeterred. "Well, that's one way to approach it I suppose. This is my way." Now they were on the sidewalk in front of the house. Steven followed Roy as he walked up to the door and knocked.

"Why don't you let me do the talking," Steven said.

"I'll be fine," Roy insisted.

There were some rumblings inside the house before they heard footsteps approaching the door from the other side. It opened to a tall, lanky man who looked hardly more than a teenager. He was dressed in a t-shirt and jeans. There were piercings in his nose. He stared blankly at them. "Yeah?"

Roy spoke right up. "I'm Roger Yates and this is," he pointed to Steven, "Henny Youngman. We're from Yates Bonding, and we're looking for an adult male, 24 years old, named Sonny Taft."

"No one here named that," the kid replied.

"He's wanted on serious charges, and this is the address we have for him. We're entitled, by law, to remand him to the court. We're not leaving without him," Roy said. Steven was impressed with Roy's performance. He didn't know how much of it the kid would buy, but it sounded pretty real.

"Look, I'd like to help you, but I don't know anyone by that name."

"How many people live here?" Roy asked.

"Seven," the kid replied.

"Do you know them all? Personally?" Roy asked.

"Well, yeah, kinda. Rachel is new, but the rest I know."

"Do you own this house?"

"Rent."

"Who owns it?"

"I don't know the guy's name. We just make rent payments to Billy, and he handles paying the landlord."

"Look," Roy said, "You tell me Sonny isn't here, OK, I believe you. But I'm gonna need the names and ages of everyone who does live here," Roy said, pulling a small notepad from his pocket. *Amazing,* Steven thought.

The kid didn't seem to like this idea. "Why do you need that?" he asked.

"So I can document for the office that we came here," Roy said, "and Sonny wasn't one of the current occupants or visitors. Look, I don't want to hassle you with a warrant, going through everything in the house. I'd hate to put you through that if he isn't here."

That flipped a switch in the kid. He rattled off the names of the residents, and Roy dutifully noted each name in the pad.

"OK," Roy told him. "If Sonny should show up, I urge you to have him contact me. It will go much easier for him if he works with us."

"Uh, OK," the kid stammered. "You got a card or something?"

"Fresh out," Roy told him, putting the pad away. "Yates Bonding. We're in the book."

The book? Steven winced, but coming from an old man the kid might believe it.

"Now before we go," Roy told the kid, "we're going to just do a quick walk around the outside of the house and then we'll be out of your hair."

"Uh, sure. OK."

Roy turned to leave the front porch, Steven following him. He waved a "bye" to the kid, who closed the door.

As they rounded the corner of the house, Steven said, "I gotta hand it to you, that was masterful."

"Thank you," Roy said. "Your old man knows how to do a thing or two."

"Henny Youngman?"

"It was the first thing that came to mind," Roy said. "That cell phone of yours take pictures?"

Steven wrestled it from his pocket and started snapping photos as they moved around the house. In back was an overgrown yard and rusted iron lawn furniture. The small lawn was mossy. There were cement steps leading up to a screen door, and a wooden basement access door with a padlock and chain through the handles. They continued around to the other side of the house, but were stopped by a wooden fence overgrown with ivy, so they backtracked to leave the yard the way they came in, Steven leading.

As they were approaching the front yard, Steven heard Roy call his name, and he turned to see Roy down on one knee, his hands out to his sides to brace himself if he fell further. *Shit*, Steven thought, *I shouldn't have brought him. He doesn't have the strength. This isn't fair to him.* "Steven," Roy called again.

Steven rushed to Roy's side. "Are you all right?" he asked, grabbing Roy's shoulder, steadying him.

"Just dizzy, that's all," Roy replied.

"Can I help?" said a man who kneeled down by Roy's other side, grabbing his shoulder. It seemed to Steven the man had come out of thin air. He was about Steven's size, with dark hair and a full beard. "Do you need to lie down? Maybe some water?"

"No, no, I'm fine, just need to get my bearings," Roy said, not yet attempting to stand, but with enough of his wits to refuse help.

The man looked at Steven and could see Steven's concern, both for his father and for who this stranger was. "I live next door," he told Steven. "I saw your father fall."

Steven didn't like him – it was an immediate visceral reaction, but for the moment he was helping and his attention returned to Roy. "Can you walk, Dad? Should I call for help?"

"No, I don't need help," Roy said, struggling to his feet. "Help me up, will you?"

"Let's get you to the car," Steven said, holding Roy's arm as they took a step.

"Please come over," the man said. "Just a few steps this way, you can sit down and have some water. Regain your strength."

While Steven was considering the offer, the man pulled Roy's arm and Roy took a step in the direction of the neighbor's house. Steven decided to go along. The car was half a block away, and having his father sit for a few minutes before they walked to it might be a good idea. The ground was flat and easy to navigate, and after a few steps they emerged into the neighbor's back yard. They sat Roy down on a bench by the house.

"Let me get some water for him, I'll be right back," the man said, and disappeared into the house.

"You OK, Dad? Really?" Steven asked.

"Yeah, I'm OK," Roy replied. "Something's up with this guy, though," he said, motioning to the stranger's house.

"Yeah, I don't like him," Steven said.

"Let's just see where this goes," Roy said. The man emerged from the house with two glasses of water in hand. He sat one down by Steven, and then handed the other glass directly to Roy.

"Thank you," Roy said, and took a sip.

"No problem at all," the man said. "I just hope you're feeling better."

"Yes, thank you for your help," Steven offered. "I'm Steven and this is my father Roy."

The man's focus remained on Roy. "Oh, no problem really, glad to help. I'm Michael."

Roy took another sip, and seemed to sit up a bit more. "You lived here long, Michael?" Roy asked.

"About twenty years. Great neighborhood."

Awkward silence. Steven felt he should say something. "We were just admiring the house next door. They told us we could take a few pictures."

"Ah, yes, it's a nice house, isn't it?" Michael said.

"Yes, impressive," said Roy. "Victorian, right?

"Correct."

Steven noticed the color had returned to Roy's face, and he looked better.

"Could use some work, though," Roy said. "Did the previous owners keep it in better condition?" Steven smiled that Roy had gone right back to work, digging for answers.

"Yes, the previous owner kept it in perfect condition. Beautiful paint job. It would stop people on the street. Cars would stop and look. But," Michael sighed, "he disappeared one day, and the place hasn't been the same since. I understand the renters are supposed to do the yard work, but they're rather lazy I'm afraid. Would you like some more water, Roy? Maybe something to eat, or some orange juice? You are looking better."

"No thank you, I am feeling fine, thanks," said Roy. "It's a shame when a house goes downhill like that. Can take all the properties around it down with it. You say he just disappeared?"

Michael seemed wistful. "Yes, no explanation, just disappeared."

"Did you know his name?" Roy pressed.

"No, why?" Michael replied.

"Oh, it's not important. Thought maybe I'd research the house a little bit. It's a hobby of mine. You know, Steven, I'm feeling much better. I think we could go now."

"Are you sure?" Michael asked. "You're welcome to stay here as long as you'd like."

"No, I'm good," Roy said, rising, and handing the empty glass back to Michael. Their eyes met for a split second, and Michael said, "Well I hope you continue to feel better. Can I help you to your car?"

"No need," Roy said. "I'm feeling perfectly fine, and I've got Steven here if I need him."

Roy turned to walk out of the yard. Steven turned to Michael and thanked him for his help. He followed Roy out of the yard, watching Roy's footing for any signs he might still be weak and lose his balance. They walked to the car in silence, as dusk turned to night and the streetlights popped on.

Once in the car, Roy turned to Steven.

"The guy is a liar."

"Really? What did he lie about?" Steven asked.

"Not knowing the guy's name. He knew him. He lied about not knowing what happened to him. He knows exactly what happened. And I swear to god, there was something in the water."

"I didn't taste anything," Steven said.

"I didn't either, but it was like drinking a restorative. I feel like a million bucks. He put something in my water."

"Now you're getting paranoid," Steven said.

"I'm telling you, he was lying," Roy insisted. "He knows a lot more than he was saying."

"How could you tell?" Steven asked.

"I could feel it," Roy replied.

Steven sighed. Normally this type of response he would completely discount, but with the events he'd experienced with his father over the past few days, he'd learned to not be so hasty with dismissals. "So what then? What do we do?"

"I think we should come back and check the house," Roy said, "when the kids are away."

"What, break in?" Steven asked.

"Yeah. Break in," Roy said. "Based on their ages and this neighborhood, I'd say they're all college students, there's a good chance they'll be gone during the day. We stake it out tomorrow morning, and once they've all left, we sneak in."

"And how are we going to do that?" Steven asked.

"The basement door. It's chained, and I got a bolt cutter at home."

Thirteen

Steven and Roy sat in the car for over two hours, sipping coffee from a thermos, as they watched each of the house residents leave. Roy ticked off a name each time someone left. As the last one closed and locked the front door, Roy said, "That's it. That's the last one."

"Unless some of them had guests over," Steven said.

"We'll be quiet about it," Roy said. "The basement doors weren't visible from any of the windows in the house. The back yard was completely overgrown. If we're careful no one will hear or see us."

They walked up the street, checking for passing cars and pedestrians. When they could see no one, they slipped along the ivy wall, and Steven helped Roy over the fence. They weren't going to risk running into the neighbor.

Roy used the bolt cutter on the chain, and quietly removed it from the door's handles. Roy lifted the right door up, and its metal hinges squeaked from lack of use.

"Slower!" Steven hissed.

Even at its slowest, the hinges still creaked. When it was open wide enough for him to slip in, Roy passed the handle to Steven and went down the steps. Steven slipped in and slowly closed the door behind him.

There were cobwebs everywhere, and a second set of doors at the bottom of six steps. Steven pointed his flashlight at the doors while Roy examined them.

"Locked?" Steven asked.

Roy reached out to the door's handle and turned. "Nope," he said. He pushed the door open.

The basement was dark but completely open. It had two windows high up near its ceiling on either side. It was unfinished, with no walls and no ceiling, just the exposed floor joists from the level above. In the middle was a staircase leading up into the house, with a closed door at the top. Steven could see daylight coming from under the door. There were stacks of boxes in corners, and a washer and dryer. By the washer was a relatively new electrical panel. In a few minutes, Steven and Roy had mentally mapped out the room.

"What are we looking for?" Steven whispered.

"Anything," Roy whispered back. "Anything unusual that might help us."

They looked deeper into the corners, under the stairs, and around the stacks of boxes. Steven took pictures with his cell phone.

"These boxes belong to the kids upstairs," said Steven. "DVDs, books, all recent. I don't see any point in going through their stuff."

"I don't either," said Roy.

Steven stumbled as his toe hit something on the cement floor. He shined his light at the floor, noticing a different texture. Roy walked over to where Steven was standing. "Look," he told Roy, "that part over there is old, you can tell by how smooth it is, probably poured a hundred years ago when the house was built. But this part here is recent, it's rougher." He followed the new cement with his light until he found an edge, and then attempted to determine the size of it by following the edge as far as it would go. "It's roughly five by five, I'd say. Hold your flashlight on it, Dad, I want to get a picture."

"Wonder what's under it?" Roy asked.

"Children's bodies?" Steven guessed, snapping photos. "Maybe Lukas himself?"

"I don't know," Roy said, "I think it's worth finding out."

"We haven't got anything to dig into it with," Steven said.

"I was thinking a trance," Roy said.

"Here? What if all hell breaks loose? We're not even sure the house is empty upstairs."

"Listen," Roy said, "we're here. Let's try. I'm not summoning Ben or the shadow, I'm just trying to find out what's under this slab."

Steven considered it. "OK, but if anything goes wrong, I'm going to physically haul you out those doors and we're getting out of here."

"Agreed," Roy said.

Roy stood over the cement patch Steven had identified. He lowered his head, and took several deep breaths. Steven watched as his father entered the trance. He was much closer to him this time than he had been for the previous trances in the hallway, and he was glad; if his father fell, he'd be much more able to catch him. Something about it still bothered him, didn't sit right with him. Here was a man he had known his whole life, about to engage in something Steven fundamentally felt was ridiculous. Even though he'd seen and experienced some completely inexplicable things in the past few days, there was a part of him that still believed they were all explainable, just not in the heat of the moment. When it was all said and done, he'd be able to look back on it all and come up with a rational explanation that didn't rely on trances, shadows, and ghosts to make sense – he just wasn't able to come up with those answers while things were moving so fast. Holding onto that belief was what made him feel sane; that if he were to just jump into things the way Roy was doing now, he'd be betraying something within himself. Maybe it was just stubbornness, but Steven knew it was there, and a part of him was uncomfortable that his dad so completely believed it that he would jump in the raging river like this without a moment's concern for the implausibility of it all.

After several minutes, Roy raised his head.

"Yes?" Steven asked. "Anything?"

"Nothing. I don't sense a thing."

"Great, where does that leave us? Digging through this cement?"

"First I think we should talk to Michael," Roy said.

"Michael? The neighbor?" Steven asked. "Why him?"

"Because," Roy said, "he's been watching us through that window."

◊

When they emerged from the basement, Michael was nowhere to be seen. Roy carefully rearranged the chain and lock to look as though it was still intact, and then they both walked next door.

Steven knocked on the door. "What are we going to say?" he asked.

"I'm not sure," Roy replied. "Let's see what *he* says."

Michael opened the door and smiled at them both. "Steven. Roy. How nice to see you both again. Please, come in."

Roy and Steven stepped through the door and into the living room. It was utilitarian. No television, no media of any kind. Just a sofa, a couple of chairs and a coffee table.

"Please, sit down," Michael motioned. "Can I get you something? Water, maybe, Roy?"

"Yes, thank you, that would be nice," Roy said. As Michael turned to leave the room and Roy moved to a chair, Steven shot him a look. Roy gave him a reassuring wink.

Michael returned, again setting a glass down for Steven, but handing a glass directly to Roy. "Here you are. It's good to see you looking better Roy."

"Well, I thank you for your concern," Roy said. "We wanted to thank you for yesterday, and we were hoping to get some more photographs of the house next door during the day, with better light."

"You seem really interested in the house," Michael said. "Are you thinking of buying it?"

He doesn't know that we saw him watching us, Steven thought. *Or, he's pretending that he didn't. Maybe he thinks we didn't identify him.*

"Maybe," Roy said. "My son and I have restored several houses over the years, and this one really caught our eye," Roy smiled, and took a sip. He immediately felt a jolt of euphoria.

"Well, I wonder if the owner would sell it," Michael said. "He's had it for a long time."

"Do you know how I might reach him?" Roy asked.

"No, I don't, I'm sorry," Michael replied. "I see the kids coming and going, and for the most part they stay to themselves. They're renters, so there's new ones every few months. Lots of bedrooms in that house. But I can't think of the last time I saw the owner. Don't know if I'd even recognize him." Michael beamed at them.

"Well, it's no matter at the moment," Roy said. "I think we're more admiring the architecture right now than anything else."

"We can always ask the kids where they send their rent checks," Steven offered.

Silence. Steven could tell Michael was uncomfortable.

"I guess I should come clean with both of you," Michael offered. "I'm the landlord of the house."

"Oh, really?" Roy said, feigning surprise. "Why didn't you want to tell us that?"

"Well, forgive me for that," Michael replied, "but I guess I wanted to know your intentions before letting on about it."

"Oh I see," Roy muttered, chuckling. "You must be an excellent negotiator. That, or you're not interested in selling the house."

"I can assure you," Michael said, "the house isn't for sale."

"Even if we were to make you a substantial offer?" Steven volunteered, wanting to see how far this would go.

"No, it's not for sale for any amount of money. It has a sentimental value that, well, can't be priced," Michael smiled.

Roy was right, Steven thought. *This guy is playing us.*

"Well," interjected Roy, "in light of that, I suppose we should be going. It was good of you to humor us at least."

"Oh, the pleasure was mine," said Michael, turning to Roy. "Can I get you anything else before you go? I just made an early lunch, why don't you join me?"

"Thank you for the offer," Steven said, "but we have an appointment we must make." They all moved towards the door.

"If you're in the neighborhood again, please stop by and say hello. It was nice to see you both. Stay healthy, Mr. Hall," he said to Roy.

"Thank you, and thanks for your hospitality." Roy turned and he and Steven left the house, returning to their car parked down the street. Once they were out of earshot, Roy began to snicker. "What kind of landlord doesn't call the cops when he sees them break into his property?"

"The kind," Steven answered, "that doesn't want cops around."

"Do you believe anything he said?" Roy asked.

"Not a word," Steven replied. "I don't know if he's the landlord or not. He sure seems fixated on you, though. And I don't believe we ever told him our last name."

"I think he's protecting something," Roy said.

"Protecting what?" Steven asked. "The bones in the basement? We don't even know if there *are* bones in the basement."

"Maybe," said Roy. "Like I told you, he's lying, hiding things."

They got in the car. Steven started it up, and drove them out of the neighborhood, back to Roy's place.

"When he said the house had sentimental value to him, he's referring to Lukas," Roy said.

"He told us the previous owner disappeared," Steven said.

"To the rest of us, Lukas disappeared. But Michael knows exactly what happened to him; he died, in that house."

"OK, so he died," Steven said. "Then this guy buys the property, end of story. This might be a dead end."

"But Lukas didn't die. Not completely, as we know," Roy said. "I think Michael knows that. I think he knows Lukas lives, in some way, and Michael is keeping watch on that house for a reason. I think he expects him back."

"Fifteen years is a long time to wait," said Steven.

"Not if you're expecting eternity out of it," Roy answered.

Fourteen

The rain came off and on that afternoon, with few sunbreaks. It was pouring by the time Steven reached Roy's house, and he grabbed an umbrella from the back seat, handing it to Roy as he prepared to step out of the car.

"I don't need that," Roy said. "I've been getting my head wet here for seventy years."

"Fine, I'll use it myself," Steven said, and popped it open outside of the car, trying to shield himself from as much rain as possible. Roy scampered to the front door and unlocked it, and Steven followed him inside, shaking the water off the umbrella before entering. Roy put on a pot of coffee.

"I don't feel like we're making much progress," Steven said.

"Oh, I think we found out quite a bit," Roy said. "And I've got a theory forming. Ben was right, Lukas wasn't human. We saw that in the flow. And, therefore, I don't think the shadow of Lukas is a ghost. I think it's something else entirely."

"What makes you think that?"

"Because it doesn't behave like a ghost. It drained Ben, and it's draining me. That's more parasitic, like a mental vampire. And it's far too powerful. What the shadow did to you and me put Ben's ghosts to shame. Ben could make things appear, but Lukas could physically move you, hold you down, harm you. Ben was human, and his ghost lingers for a reason – to warn us about Lukas, about Ben's unfinished business. Lukas was undergoing some kind of metamorphosis; that takes energy. The shadow is a projection of himself, at the only level he is able to function at right now, in his current state. It's not a ghost."

"So wherever he's buried right now," Steven asked, "he's...functional."

"To some degree."

"Then why attack you? What is Lukas after?"

"I think what he takes from me," Roy said, "he's using to continue his metamorphosis, or to stay alive in the grave long enough to find a way to continue."

"And we're helping him. We keep offering you up, and he's using what he takes from you to try and return. No more séances, no more trances."

"Too late," Roy said, "we've engaged, the connection has been made. He knows me now, he views me as food. He'll keep coming after me until he wipes me out, just like Ben. My fate was sealed the moment I walked into your house."

"We know how to keep him at bay. We just have to sleep in shifts."

"For the rest of my life?" said Roy. "I don't think so."

There was silence. A wave of guilt washed over him. Had he not involved his father three days ago, his father wouldn't be in this position. Of course, he hadn't known the consequences at the time, or he wouldn't have. And his father had practically insisted. But he had invited him over to witness the occurrences. That was when the connection was made. Steven could still see the shadow and its eyes staring at Roy, sleeping in bed, floating an inch off the mattress, being slowly drained to feed the corpse of Lukas Johansen.

"Dad, I'm sorry," he said. "If I hadn't asked you to come over…"

"Nah," Roy said, "you're viewing this the wrong way, you always do. You didn't push me into the river, I jumped in. It's always my choice to jump, never anyone else's." Roy poured himself more coffee. "We just have to find this sonofabitch and finish the job."

◊

Steven spent the afternoon doing more research, leaving his father at home with a promise that he would rest but not sleep. They would do shift-sleeping again that night. Until then, he wanted to follow up on a couple of ideas.

His first stop was at the construction office of a buddy of his named Ned Tate. Ned was a small subcontractor who worked on house construction. Ned and Steven had known each other since college. At one time Steven thought Ned might have had a thing for Sheryl, and in retrospect he wouldn't put it past her to throw herself at him. Still, Ned had always remained a good family friend. He had last seen him at

Ned's daughters' college graduation. Steven found him onsite in a new housing subdivision in Maple Valley, a forty-five minute drive outside of Seattle.

Steven sat down at Ned's dirty desk in the construction trailer. There were receipts and canary colored work orders all over it, a couple coffee mugs with yesterday's (or older) coffee, and an engraved plaque that read "No Whining."

"I'm hoping you can tell me how I might figure out what's under a slab of concrete," Steven said.

"That's easy," said Ned. "Jackhammer."

"Eh, I can't really go that route. I can't tear it up, not yet. I need to find out if there's something under it before I tear it up."

Ned's eyebrows rose. "Well, you could use a GPR."

"What's that?" Steven asked.

"It's like an x-ray machine, for underground," Ned answered. "We use them to check for pipes and conduits before we dig. What are you looking for?"

"Well, it's kind of hard to explain," said Steven. "Here, take a look at this, would you?" Steven handed his cell phone to Ned, displaying a picture of the cement floor inside the Victorian house. "What if I wanted to x-ray under that? Would it work? Would it show me if something was under there?"

"Sure, I don't see why not. You're not going to tell me why?"

"Not yet Ned, I really can't. Trust me. But can you tell me, would it detect..." Steven paused. He didn't know if he should go any further.

"Detect what?" Ned asked, his interest clearly piqued.

No, too risky, Steven thought. He couldn't say "bones" without the conversation wheeling off in the wrong direction. "...a gas line? Would it detect a gas line?" he stammered.

"Yeah, sure. That's one of the reasons we use it," Ned said, still examining the photo. "But if you dig here you'll want to be careful of the sump pump."

"A sump pump?" Steven asked.

"Yeah," Ned replied. "This looks like a French drain to me. Very common in old homes in Seattle. When it rains and the ground gets soaked, most old basements built before fifty years ago will flood. To solve that, you put in a French drain with a sump pump, keeps the basement dry. That's what it looks like to me, done maybe ten, fifteen years ago. I wouldn't dig it up to find that out if it's working fine. And you sure as hell don't need to pay to rent a GPR. I can loan you ours if it comes to that."

Steven let this roll around in his head, and he liked it. He found a straightforward plausible answer refreshing, even if it wasn't the one he'd expected. "Thanks Ned," he said, grabbing his cell phone back. "I appreciate the advice. I might take you up on the GPR down the road. Let's get together for a beer soon," he said, as he backed toward the trailer door.

"Sure, no problem buddy," Ned said, watching him go. A worker approached him with a question and Ned's attention turned back to his work.

Steven picked up Roy and he drove them both to Steven's house. On the way he explained what Ned had told him.

"Lukas' house is a bust. You felt nothing standing over the patch, and Ned says it's a sump pump. If Ben killed him, he didn't bury him there, especially with that nosy freak next door. If he buried him at all. This is all just a wild theory."

"Oh, he buried him," Roy said. "I'll bet every penny I have on it."

"You're sure of that?" Steven asked.

"Absolutely," Roy replied.

"OK," Steven continued, "then where would he bury him? Some place where he had enough privacy to do it. My place, Ben's old house. He could take his time doing it."

"The shadow did appear there first," Roy said.

"Well, you tried to 'feel' whether there was anything under the patch in the basement at Lukas's house when we snuck in. Are you sure that method works? Can you detect things that way?"

"I think so," Roy said.

"Think?" Steven asked. "Or know?"

"Think," Roy said. "Just think. Nothing is perfect, you know. I can't guarantee it. I knew where Ben's journal was hidden, didn't I?"

"Yeah," said Steven. "That's good enough for me. I figure we'll walk you over every square inch at my place. Like a divining rod. See if anyplace triggers you. If Lukas is buried there it ought to set you off like a pinball machine."

Fifteen

Steven and Roy performed a quick survey of the house, basement and back yard before beginning.

"Let's do the basement first," Steven suggested. "Now, if you go into the trance can I move you? Can you walk?"

"Of course I can walk," Roy said. "Let's give it a trial run and see."

"So, what, you go into a trance, then I lead you around?"

"Yeah."

"How will you know if you've detected something?" Steven asked.

"I'll know," Roy replied. "And I'll tell you. Some things are harder to detect than others, but Lukas isn't subtle. The problem will be the walking. My vision won't be focused on things on the floor."

"Why don't you put your arm on the back of my shoulder, like this," Steven said, demonstrating, "and then I can lead you around by walking, and you just follow me."

"Fine by me," Roy replied. "When do we start?"

"Let's try it now," Steven said, leading him to the downstairs family room. It had the most recent remodeling of any room in the house, and Steven thought it the most likely suspect.

They paced over all of the room, Steven leading Roy slowly, going back and forth across the room in two foot increments. Steven resisted the urge to ask his father if he was feeling anything. He couldn't see Roy's face, so he didn't know if some areas of the room brought about some reaction more than others. When they finally reached the end of the room, he turned to face Roy.

"Anything?"

"Nope."

"Really?"

"I said no."

"Not even a slight bump?"

"What's a slight bump?" Roy asked.

"You know, something that made your meter jump a little?"

"Meter? I don't know what you think I'm doing, but there's no meter involved."

"I didn't mean it literally. Something that...impressed you...more than normal?"

"And I told you, no."

The pattern again. Time to back off.

"Shit. I thought this room might be it."

"Well, let's try another room," Roy said.

They moved to one of the bedrooms and repeated the procedure, with the same result. Then they tried the bathroom, the hallways, and laundry room.

"Nothing," Roy said.

"The backyard is private," Steven said. "We can scan it this way without people seeing us. Let's go."

For the next hour they slowly paced over every square inch of the yard, Steven careful not to interrupt his father and mindful of uneven surfaces. Towards the end he could tell Roy was tiring, his breathing was increasing and his pace slowing.

They finished the last pass against the back fence, and Steven turned to Roy. "Anything?"

Roy just shook his head. "I could use a beer," he said.

Steven followed him into the house, retrieved the beers, and they drank together in the kitchen.

"So?" Steven said.

"So," Roy replied, "he's not buried here."

"You're sure?"

"Not one hundred percent, but yes, I'm sure."

"Because," Steven said, "if he was, you'd have felt something, right?"

"Yes, goddamnit!" Roy snapped. He was obviously tired and Steven's questions were irritating him.

"Maybe you were tired out there, maybe your tuner wasn't...fully powered. Maybe we should try again when you've got more energy."

"It won't make any difference, he's not out there," Roy replied.

"Fine," Steven said. "So, if not here, where?"

"I don't know where. But I can tell you, it's not here, and it's not at the Lukas house. We're wasting our time at either place."

Steven was scraping the barrel for answers. "We could go back to Michael. Confront him with our theory."

Roy considered this. "Maybe."

"He's involved, we know that," Steven said. "You said he knows more than he told us. He's hiding something. If we tell him we're on to him, it might rattle him, we might shake some information from him."

"Doesn't feel right," Roy said.

"Feel right?" Steven asked. "What does that mean? He knows more about this than we do, more than he's let on. And we need to find out what he knows. Seems simple."

"It means," said Roy, "that it feels wrong. Something's wrong with that approach. I can't tell you why. It just doesn't feel correct."

"Well," said Roy, "unless you have a better idea, that's my next stop."

"Wait," Roy said. "I'll go with you. But we need to stop at my place first."

"Why?"

"Because there's something I need to get, first."

"What?"

"Jesus Christ with the third degree!"

"No secrets, Dad. I want to know what you're planning. I don't want you going off on some agenda that I don't know about. If we're going to confront this guy, I want us both to be on the same page."

"Agreed," said Roy. "I want to pick up something that will give us some protection."

"What, like a talisman or something?"

"Kind of like that, yes."

"You think we need protection from this guy?" Steven asked.

"Yes," Roy replied, "I do. I told you it seems wrong. Anything that might tilt things to our advantage, yes, we should consider."

"You think he's dangerous? You think when we tell him what we suspect he'll come unglued?"

"Yes, I think there's a good chance of that."

When they reached Roy's place, Steven sat in the living room while Roy disappeared into the back. He emerged carrying a 9mm pistol, which he flashed at Steven with a smile, then tucked into his coat pocket.

"That's your talisman?" Steven asked.

"God bless America," Roy replied, rummaging through a kitchen cabinet.

"I thought we were going to pick up some trinket that would protect us from evil powers, but your plan is to shoot the guy."

"Best protection money can buy," Roy called to him, as he located a bottle in the cabinet and returned to Steven. "That, and this." He showed Steven the bottle.

It was a small Mason jar. Inside was an inch of clear liquid.

"I'm afraid to ask, but what is it?" Steven said.

"Hasn't got a name," Roy replied, opening it. "I whipped it up a couple of days ago. Old habits die hard, I hid it in the back of the kitchen cabinets, afraid Claire would find it. Guess I could have just left it out here on the counter."

"What do you mean," Steven asked, "you whipped it up?"

"It's from the book," Roy said. "Protection."

"Protection?" Steven asked, incredulous. "What is this, a potion from your secret book? You've got to be kidding me."

"And you're telling me," Roy replied, "that after everything you've seen the past few days you think the idea of some extra protection is silly?"

"The gun I buy," Steven said, "the potion is bullshit."

"Fine, then none for you. But you should know this stuff has been keeping me going the past few days."

"What do you mean?"

"I mean," replied Roy, "that without it, I'd be in a hospital bed by now. Lukas would have drained much more than he's been able to."

"What does it do?" Steven asked.

"Never you mind, it's bullshit, remember?" Roy shot back sarcastically.

"Fine, you drink it, and you feel empowered, protected, whatever. Can't hurt."

"Exactly."

"What's in it?"

"You don't need to know."

"I do if it's poisonous."

"If it was poisonous, why would I drink it? Besides, you're not going to drink any."

Steven sighed. The pattern could go on and on, he was always the one who had to break it.

"Do you drink it now, or take it with us and drink it there?" Steven asked.

"I'll drink it now, provided we're going straight over to talk to him."

"That's the plan."

Roy downed the remaining liquid in the jar and replaced the cap. "Let's go."

◊

Lights were on at the small house next to the Victorian mansion. Steven and Roy had discussed their plan on the ride over. Steven would lay down the theory, and Roy would press him for more information. They didn't need to tell him everything they knew, or guessed, just enough to upset him and hopefully cause him to divulge more information. Roy would keep the gun ready if things got out of hand.

Steven knocked, and they waited nervously. A moment later, Michael opened the door.

"Gentlemen!" he said, enthusiastically. "Come in! Good to see you both again!"

They walked inside, and he motioned for them to sit on the furniture in the living room. "Please, sit, can I get you anything? Would you like some tea, or some water?"

"No, we're fine," said Steven. Michael turned to look at Roy, seeming to want a confirmation from Roy that he didn't want anything either. Roy shook his head.

"Well then, what can I do for you?" Michael asked.

"Well," Steven started, "we were hoping you could shed some light on a few problems we're having."

"I'd be delighted to help any way I can," Michael replied.

"Thank you for that, I think you're just the man to help us," Steven said. "We could really use some more information about the house next door."

"Ah, the house again. What is it?"

Steven looked Michael in the eye.

"This is just a theory of ours, and I know this might sound crazy, but both I and my father believe that the former resident of the house, fifteen years back, might have been responsible for the disappearance of several young children in the neighborhood."

A chill fell upon the room. He looked in Michael's eyes for any kind of deflection or evasion, but there was none.

"Doesn't sound crazy at all," Michael replied.

Steven was taken back. "So," he started, "you think Lukas Johansen might have been responsible for those disappearances?"

"I don't think so," Michael said, "I know so." He turned his head to Roy. "Just as you know, Roy."

Steven turned to look at Roy, who was staring back at Michael. Steven felt there was something passing between them, and he was suddenly glad that Roy had downed the protection before they left.

"Ours is a theory," Steven said, trying to keep the plan moving forward. "But it sounds like you might have witnessed something back then?"

"I did," Michael said, returning his gaze to Steven. "I helped him consume them."

Dead silence. Steven felt a little numb, unsure how to react. This was not the direction he thought things would go. He felt sweat break out on the back of his neck, and he braced himself, half expecting Michael to bolt across the room and attack him. He glanced over to Roy and could see Roy was on full alert, his hand in his coat pocket. He knew that inside, Roy had the gun aimed at Michael.

"Consume them?" Steven asked.

"Yes," Michael said, matter-of-factly. "I captured each of them, prepared them for him, and then we consumed them together."

"A ritual?" Roy asked.

"Funny that you should ask," Michael said to Roy, "when you already know. But I suppose you ask for his benefit," he said, returning to Steven. "He seems a little slow."

Steven was grasping for the next thing to say that would keep the plan working, but it was clearly failing. He was hoping to shake up Michael, but the reverse was happening. "I guess my next stop should be the police," Steven said.

"You'll need some evidence, or it will turn out like your last interaction with them," Michael said, delivering another shock.

"It was you," Steven said slowly, "in my house the other night. You broke into my house?"

"And it will be over before you get any evidence," Michael continued, ignoring him.

"Not if we find the bodies of those children buried in the house next door," Steven said, trying a bluff. "The cops might be interested in digging to find out."

"Dig away, Steven. I told you, they were *consumed*," Michael emphasized in a way that made Steven sick to his stomach.

"What will be over?" Roy asked. "You said it would 'be over' before we get any evidence. What will be over?"

"What do you think, Roy?" Michael asked calmly, smiling at Roy as though he was his long-lost grandfather.

"The ritual," Roy replied. "The ritual will be over."

"If you want to call it that," Michael said.

"Do you know where Lukas is at, right now?" Steven asked.

"No. But I wish I did," Michael said sadly. "I presume Ben buried him after he killed him. He must have buried him somewhere...but where? I suppose if you could find him, you'd have your evidence, at least of one murder."

"That's the plan, isn't it?" Roy asked. "For us to find him, and dig him up."

"Is that a rhetorical question?" Michael asked, smiling.

"What is the ritual?" Steven asked.

"Don't you two talk?" Michael said. "Ask Roy. He already knows."

Steven turned to Roy, but Roy kept his gaze on Michael, and his hand on the gun in his pocket.

"I'm guessing Lukas was short a consumption or two before Ben screwed up the plan," Roy said.

"Only one," Michael said, spreading his arms, still smiling. "And I'm ready and waiting. The children are concentrated in me. Once he consumes me, we'll be eternal."

Steven saw Roy pull the gun out of his pocket. He was surprised to see him aim it at Michael, but in a moment it all clicked for him – Michael was the final step of the ritual. Michael was waiting to be consumed by Lukas, to finish the process. If Roy killed him, it might end the ritual before it could be completed.

The gun clicked, misfiring. He pulled the trigger repeatedly, with the same result.

"I'm far too big of an investment to not protect, Roy," Michael said, lowering his arms. "Four children and fifteen patient years aren't going to be dispensed by an old man and his thick son, regardless of how protected you are."

Roy lowered the gun, returned it to his pocket. For a moment they all sat looking at each other in a sort of stalemate.

"What now?" Steven said.

"Well, I think you and Roy should run along and figure out where Ben buried him," Michael said. "Unless you'd like something to eat first. I have a casserole in the oven, there's plenty for all of us."

"We won't do it," Steven said. "Lukas can rot in the ground."

"Then what you've experienced the last few days," said Michael, leaning forward towards Steven, "will be nothing compared to what will come." He turned to Roy. "And you know what will happen to you."

Steven's defensiveness of Roy kicked into high gear at this threat, and he stood. "Come on, Dad. We're leaving."

Roy stood, and so did Michael. They all went to the door.

"Thanks for coming," Michael said. "Please let me know if there's anything else I can do to help."

Steven shot a glance at Roy. He looked as angry as he'd ever seen him, as though he wanted to deck Michael, but knew better. They walked out of the house without a word and to their car, hearing Michael shut the door behind them.

◊

They returned to Roy's house, not saying much. Roy walked down the hallway to his bedroom, and returned with a large book that he dropped on the kitchen table in front of Steven. "There," he said, pointing to it. "The answer is in there, somewhere. Just gotta find it."

"Is this it?" Steven asked. "The secret book?"

"Yup," Roy replied. "That's it. Secret no longer. See if *you* can figure it out."

"I wouldn't know where to start," Steven said. "And I'm not sure I want to."

Roy sat next to Steven. "Well, I'm not sure we have a choice," he said.

"You always say we always have a choice," Steven responded. "We could just drop the whole thing, not play into these assholes."

"That's true," Roy replied. "In this case, I think that choice is a bad choice if I want to keep living."

Steven lowered his head. He thought for a moment he might cry, just lose it from all the strangeness and stress. He was just a normal guy who didn't believe in abnormal things. Not only was his job gone, his house had indeed turned out to be unlivable. But the thing that really pushed him to the edge was his father's life being used as ransom to locate and dig up a monster. They were being forced to play out a terrible scenario and the unfairness of it ate into him like acid.

"Funny," Roy said, "in most hauntings, once you solve the mystery of why the ghosts are there, the problem is solved. In this case, it just made things worse."

"All ghost stories are solved by finding out what is unknown, right?" Steven asked.

"Usually," replied Roy. "And then setting things straight."

"Well, what we don't know is how to kill this fucker," said Steven, changing his resolve. "We just have to find that out, and then kill him to set things right. That will stop the ritual, the metamorphosis. Lukas will be dead and gone, and he'll leave you alone. That should make Ben happy, too, get him to shut up. Then I can go back home, have a decent night's sleep, and you can return to whatever you were doing before I wrapped you up in this."

Roy mulled this over. "What about Michael?"

"He'll be inert."

"Well," said Roy, "it's all academic until we find where Lukas is buried."

"And," added Steven, "we know how to kill him correctly."

Sixteen

Third time's the charm, Steven thought as he pulled his car into the trailer park and wormed his way to trailer number 48. He parked and waited until 7 p.m. He had considered calling Debra, but didn't want to reach John and get her into trouble with him for having talked to him.

He glanced down the street towards her space and didn't see John's truck there. He wanted to get back to Roy as soon as possible. He decided to walk up to Debra's now, rather than wait the additional half hour for John to leave. Besides, it looked like Debra's husband had already gone to work.

He walked up to the trailer door and knocked. At the same time the door opened, a man walked from around the back of the trailer. Both Debra at the door and John from the corner of the trailer said "Hello?" at the same time.

"Uh, sorry, I thought maybe…" he said to Debra, unsure how to finish. Her face looked crestfallen. John couldn't see her from where he stood, and she tried to get Steven to leave by silently waving her hand at the wrist, like she was shooing away a bug. She mouthed the word, "go!" Or maybe it was "no!" Steven couldn't be sure.

"Yes, what do you want?" John asked, stepping closer to Steven and into Debra's view.

Steven stared at him. *I fucked up,* Steven thought. *He must not have a shift tonight. Where the fuck is his truck?* John ran all the options through his mind as quickly as he could, and settled on honesty.

"Steven Hall," he said, extending his hand. "I called you several days back."

John stared at him blankly while shaking his hand, obviously not recalling.

"Regarding your father."

John let the hand drop. "I don't have anything to say to you. Go on, get."

Go on, get? Steven thought. *Did he just tell me to 'get'?*

"I don't want to bother you," Steven said, "trust me, I wouldn't be here if it wasn't important."

"You're already bothering me," John said. "I told you I didn't want to speak to you, and you come to my home anyway? Are you stalking me? Why shouldn't I call the cops?"

"Because my father is in trouble," Steven said, looking at him. "Just like Ben was. The exact same thing." He could see him soften a little, so Steven decided to pursue it and see if he could win him over. "And I'm desperate for any little thing that might help him. I would not have come here if I didn't believe my father's life was in jeopardy."

At this John seemed to soften even more. He appeared to be considering it, rather than going for his shotgun to run him off.

"Please," Steven pleaded. "I don't know who else to ask."

Debra spoke up from the trailer doorway. "John, why don't you give this man five minutes? His father is in trouble, and it's the Christian thing to do."

John seemed to be mulling this over. Eventually he sighed and said, "All right. Five minutes. What do you want from me?"

"Thank you," Steven said. He then asked John some of the same questions he'd already run past Debra, but he left out their theory about Ben killing Lukas. John gave him answers similar to what he'd heard from Debra. Sooner or later he'd lose John's patience. He was going to have to hit him with the big question he'd driven out to ask Debra in the first place, but without telling him about the shadow and the child killings. He was afraid it would come out of left field and put John off. He decided to soften him up even more first.

"My father started assisting me a few days ago, and from how you've described Ben, my father is experiencing the same problems. I had to take him to the ER the other night. I'm truly afraid for his life."

"I'm sorry to hear that," John said. "I wouldn't wish what happened to my dad on anyone else."

"This may sound like a crazy question John, but it's really important to me figuring this thing out," Steven said. "When Ben started to go downhill, did he ever mention a place other than his home? Did he have any property somewhere?"

"He didn't mention anything, but we have a family cabin south of Leavenworth," John said. "It's been in our family for generations. I know Ben went there a couple of times before he died. He loved it there. Why?"

"I'm not sure yet," Steven said. "Would you mind if I visited there? Not to stay or anything, just to check out a theory I've got? It might help explain what's been happening."

John looked down at his feet, then over at Debra. "You going to tell me why?"

Steven looked down, stammered. "You'd just think I'm crazy."

John paused. "Maybe not," he said.

Steven looked up at him, pleading. But he wasn't going to tell the whole story to John. It was too much, it would just derail the goal, which was getting access to Ben's property for another search. There would be plenty of time to tell John all about it if it panned out. But for now, he pressed his lips shut and John took the message.

"OK," John said. "Deb, would you get the cabin keys for him?" Debra said, "Yeah," smiled, and left the doorway. John turned to Steven. "You got a pen? I'll give you directions. It isn't easy."

Steven whipped out his phone and opened a note. "Go ahead," he said. John described the route Steven would need to take to find the cabin. When he was finished, he said, "You can stay out there as long as you need. This time of year none of us go out there. There's no electricity, but there's some lanterns if you bring oil. Heat is from a wood burning stove. No hot water unless you boil it on the stove."

Debra returned with the keys, and gave them to John. He handed them to Steven. "I hope you find what you're looking for, and your dad improves," he said. "And that you can put an end to whatever this is. I've never been more scared than when I was around him in those final few weeks. It got so bad Deb wouldn't come with me to visit him. I didn't want to go either. To tell you the truth, I felt like he was murdered. If you can figure out what did that to him, and do something about it..." he began to tear up, "...I'd be extremely grateful to you. And I know it would give him peace. So bring the keys back whenever you're finished. You take care of yourself and your dad," he said, averting his eyes from Steven and turning to walk back behind the trailer.

Steven nodded his thanks to Debra. She winked back at him. He turned and walked back to his car, determined to, as John had said, put an end to this.

Seventeen

Steven and Roy left early the next morning after an evening of shift-sleeping. Steven did the driving, and Roy kept an eye on him to make sure he didn't fall asleep at the wheel, but after twenty minutes on the freeway Roy was out. Steven let him sleep. He navigated the hour and a half drive East of Seattle into the forest. Leavenworth was a small tourist town, decked out in a Bavarian theme, catering to skiers in the winter and shoppers in the summer. The highway that led south from Leavenworth was heavily used by the tourists to return to I-90, but it ran through US forest land, and had little commerce. The small roads that left the highway and wormed their way into the forest were only used by locals. Steven followed John's directions, taking several turns off one of the roads, and at the final instruction found himself at the end of a long dirt path better suited for an SUV than his Accord. If he had found the correct dirt road, the cabin would be a hundred yards further down a dirt trail to their right. He woke Roy.

"We're here?" Roy asked.

"Yeah, I think so," Steven replied. "We'll have to go down that trail to be sure."

Roy held his head as he straightened up in the seat. "Something wrong?" Steven asked.

"Headache," Roy said. "Probably slept wrong on the drive up."

"Come on," Steven said, "let's check out the trail. Maybe they have some aspirin in the cabin."

Steven retrieved a backpack from the car that he had loaded with flashlights, oil, bottled water, and the binoculars. The trees were tight in this area, and when he shut the trunk it echoed.

They walked down the path from the car. It was overgrown in some places, and mostly level.

"I imagine they have to trim this back every year," Steven said, maneuvering around small branches.

"Or not," replied Roy. "When you have a place like this, you have it because you want to be away from other people. An open, inviting path isn't considered essential. Or desirable. You'd just as soon no one know you're here, and you don't want to see anyone yourself."

"Or maybe," replied Steven, "they just like the woods, and the path grows over every year."

Roy stopped, and Steven expected him to say something acerbic. Instead, he reached his arms out, like he had at the first visit to the Victorian mansion, anticipating a fall.

"You OK?" Steven asked, moving over to him.

"Dizzy," Roy said. "Just dizzy."

"Let's wait here for a bit, until you get your bearings. Probably moving too fast after that nap."

Roy didn't object and Steven held onto him as they stood in the path, waiting for Roy to regain his stability. "Look," Steven said, "that looks like the roof of the place, up ahead."

They couldn't see the whole cabin from where they stood, but it was obvious that it was below them, and the path must wind downward ahead. Steven glanced through the woods in other directions – Roy was right, there was nothing to be seen. No other cabins, cars, or people.

"Let's go," Roy said. "I can walk."

"Do you want me to hold onto you?" Steven asked.

"No," Roy replied.

"Well, say something if you feel dizzy again," Steven said. "We're a long way from a hospital if you break a leg or a hip."

"Hmmpf," Roy replied.

Another couple of minutes, and they were standing in front of it. Some of it must have been from the first generation that built it, but many pieces were added on or replaced over the years, and it was a hodgepodge of wood types and materials. The door and door frame were newer, and Steven used the key in it while Roy held himself up against the frame. Steven observed Roy holding his head again. "Let's see what we can find in here," he said, entering the cabin.

It was one room, with an open kitchen in the back, and a single bedroom to the side, with a bathroom off that. Steven rummaged through the cabinets in the kitchen looking for something he could give Roy for the headache, but found nothing. He tried the bathroom, which contained only a toilet and a cabinet. In the cabinet he found a bottle of Tylenol. He brought it out for Roy.

"Here, take a couple of these," Steven said, pulling a bottle of water from the backpack and handing it to Roy. Roy opened the bottle and downed the medicine. "What now?" he said to Steven.

"Not sure. You feeling anything?" Steven asked.

"Just this headache," Roy replied. "It's a doozy, too."

"Let's wait until it subsides before we try anything more," Steven said. Roy sat in a chair, and Steven began looking around the cabin. "It's likely he didn't bury him in this cabin," Steven said. "Wouldn't want the grandkids to run into him. If he buried him up here, he would have buried him somewhere out there, in the woods, far enough away that no one would find the grave."

"Makes sense," said Roy. "What are we going to do, search the woods?"

"I guess we'll have to," Steven replied.

"And if we find the grave? What then?"

"I don't know. Dig down until we find the body, then use a couple of shotguns on it? No one will hear, out here."

"Now who's gun happy?" Roy said. "How do you know that wasn't Ben's approach in the first place? He might be down there riddled with holes already."

Steven was getting irritated. "I don't know. Maybe chop him into pieces."

"With what?" Roy asked. "A knife from the kitchen?"

"Listen, I'm just guessing here, trying to figure it out."

"The problem will be," Roy said, "that as soon as we've freed him from the grave, we'll be vulnerable. We have to have a foolproof way to finish him off. For now, let's just locate the grave. No digging until we have a plan." Roy stood.

"You feeling better?" Steven asked.

"A little," Roy replied. "Let's start."

They walked out the front door into the small clearing in front of the cabin.

"How do we do this?" Steven asked.

"Same as before," said Roy. "Let me hold onto your shoulder, you guide."

"I think we should start at the cabin, and circle it. Then spiral out."

"Fine."

Steven led Roy through the route he proposed, widening the spiral by a few feet each time they circled the cabin. Soon they were into the woods and needing to dodge trees, making the progress much slower. By the fifth circle, Steven could tell Roy was slowing down, but then he seemed to get his wind back and they continued on. It happened again on the sixth and seventh circles. On the eighth circuit, Steven stopped when he felt his dad slow.

"Dad," Steven said, "you slow down each time we hit this part of the circle. Are you feeling anything?"

"Just exhausted," Roy replied.

"But then you pick back up as we move on. Watch."

They kept walking, and Roy did speed up.

"Do you feel anything?"

"No, I just get dizzy for a second."

"Yeah," Steven said, "but why each time we're here? Come over here, Dad. Step right here." Steven led him back to the point in the circle when he noticed the slow down. "What do you feel now, standing right here?"

Roy paused. "Dizzy. A little nauseous. Weak."

Steven grabbed him by the shoulders and moved him a few paces away. Roy stopped, concentrated. "Better. Not dizzy. Stronger."

"Stay here, I'll be right back," Steven said. He returned to the cabin, and grabbed pieces of firewood that were stacked by the front door. As he walked back to Roy, he placed the logs at the points on the circle where Roy had seemed to falter. He placed the last log on the spot he had just tested with Roy.

"You're thinking," said Roy, "that if I follow that line away from the cabin, I'll get sicker and sicker."

"Yeah," replied Steven, "and if you step away from it, you'll feel better."

"Only one way to find out," Roy said, walking towards the last log, and pointing himself away from the cabin along the trajectory the logs formed.

Steven followed him, ready to catch him if he fell. "If it gets too bad, please stop and say something."

Roy nodded. He took a step, and then another, along the line formed by the logs. Steven watched his face. "How's it feeling?" Steven asked after they had walked about twenty feet.

"Definitely not pleasant," Roy replied.

"Let's test it again," Steven asked. "Step over here."

Roy side-stepped the path, following Steven to a spot several paces from the line. "Better," he said. "Not dizzy. I think you've discovered it."

"Or something," Steven said. They returned to the line and continued into the woods, walking another fifty feet. Steven kept his eyes on Roy's face and feet, looking for any sign of danger.

"How about now?" Steven asked.

"I feel like I have the flu," Roy said. "Very lightheaded. I think..."

Roy looked like he was going to fall over, and Steven grabbed his arm. Roy buckled and vomited.

"OK, that's enough," Steven said. "We're going back."

◊

Steven brought Roy another bottle of water. "Do you want any more of these?" he asked, shaking the bottle of pills.

Roy was laying down on the sofa in the main room of the cabin. "No. Just make me sicker. Did you check the expiration date on those?"

"What did you feel out there?" Steven asked. "Tell me what it was like. Were you being drained?"

"Not exactly," Roy answered. "Stronger in some ways, but not the same as back in town with the shadow." Roy occasionally winced while talking.

"And how is it now?" Steven asked.

"A little better," Roy said.

"You still look like you're in pain."

"I don't think it's going to get any better than this, at least as long as I'm here. I should have brought protection."

"What, the potion?" Steven scoffed.

"Yes," Roy answered sarcastically, "the potion. I didn't have time to make any more before we came."

"How about some vodka, Dad?" Steven said, lifting a bottle he found on the counter. "That'd probably work just as well."

"Maybe," Roy said, holding his head again. "It is one of the ingredients."

Steven put the bottle down, walked over to Roy.

"I'd like to follow that path, see what I can find," Steven said. "There's no way you're going any further, you're going to have to stay here. Are you OK if I go check it out?"

Roy nodded. "I'll be fine," he said. "Go. But remember, if you find it, do not dig it up until we have a plan."

"I won't," Steven said. "And I won't be long. Stay here and rest. But do not sleep."

Roy waved him away with his hand. Steven headed out the door, and to the logs.

◊

It had been several minutes since he had progressed beyond the spot where Roy had gotten sick. He brought several more logs to act as markers. It was easy to lose track of where you were in the forest, and following a straight line was impossible. You always had to go around a fallen log, or tree, or bramble, and then attempt to get back on track. It was still well before noon and if something went wrong he'd have plenty of daylight to find his way back. *This is no place to be in the dark*, he thought.

After what seemed like ten more minutes of walking, the ground began to rise, and in several places became steep enough that he had to re-think the trajectory. He hadn't gone far out of his way when he saw the opening to the cave.

Steven instinctively knew this was it. He approached the entrance, which was partially hidden by hanging moss and fallen trees. There was a small stream running out of it. He checked his watch – he'd been away from the cabin for twenty minutes – he would spend only a few more in the cave, and see if he could find anything that indicated a grave.

He stepped into the entrance, watching his footing. He looked for signs that other people had been there, but found none – no discarded beer cans or wrappers. If people came to this cave it was rare. The stream that trickled out of it was small and not more than an inch deep in places. After a few steps the light dropped dramatically and Steven retrieved a flashlight from his backpack.

The first hundred feet of the cave was not roomy. It was easy enough to keep walking, but the ceiling was only a foot or so above Steven, and claustrophobia began to set in. He looked for graffiti or carvings on the walls but there were none. After another fifty feet the light from outside the entrance wasn't visible. He felt completely isolated. The pathway continued the same forward as back. He scanned the ground for signs of disturbance or overturned earth, but the surface was smooth on either side of the stream. He continued on.

It seemed like he walked for another twenty minutes but by his watch it was only five. He was beginning to think he needed to return to his father, make sure he was all right. If he left now, it would take him at least a half hour to get back to the cabin, and Roy would have been alone for almost an hour. *What if the old man fell asleep?* he thought. *Would this proximity to Lukas's body make his attacks more potent? I shouldn't have left him.*

Just as he resolved to turn around and begin back, the tunnel opened into a small room that was the size of a large living room. Steven could see a pathway leading out at the other end. There was more water in here, in some places several inches deep. Some of the ground was exposed, and

Steven scanned it for signs of a grave. Nothing appeared obvious. *What would a grave from fifteen years ago look like in here, now?* Steven wondered.

He followed the stream and another room lay beyond, similar to the one he just left. He examined the ground there too, finding nothing that stood out to him as a grave site. The tunnel continued on into a third room. Here, he was startled to find several animal skeletons. One was large and looked canine, like a wolf.

God, what if this is a home for wolves or bears? he wondered. Bears were plentiful in this area. He suddenly thought he'd made a huge mistake coming into the cave unarmed. The ground here was more scuffed, and it looked like several holes had been dug, but by animals, not humans. The water from the stream pooled on one side of the room; Steven couldn't tell how deep it was.

Enough, he thought. *Time to return to Roy. I can always come back. Next time with Roy's 9mm or a shotgun.* He knew his dad had a wide selection of firearms. The smart thing to do was to return home and come back more prepared. Roy could make more of his potion, Steven would remember to bring painkillers, and they'd being plenty of ammo.

As Steven turned and began to backtrack, the sensation that something was following him overcame him. He stopped, turned, and looked, but nothing was there. He picked up his pace on the way out, now familiar with the terrain, but the faster he walked, the surer he became that an animal was chasing him out. A bear, or a bobcat, or maybe a wolf. The sounds of his steps echoing in the small space of the tunnel helped create the illusion. He turned several times, checking, and each time nothing was there. As he approached the cave entrance he slowed his pace a little, catching his breath. Once outside, he paused and took a swallow from a bottle of water in the backpack. He let his mind calm down, and began the trek back to the cabin. His markers were easy to find and soon he saw the cabin come into view.

He opened the door to the cabin and stepped inside. "Roy?" he called.

Roy was not on the sofa. He searched the cabin, calling for him, but he was not in any of the rooms. He walked back outside.

"Roy!" he called, and waited. No response.

Now Steven was really worried. *I shouldn't have gone for so long, not while he was feeling bad,* he thought. He circled the cabin, calling. Still no response.

He knew his father wasn't along the path to the cave. That left the path to the car. Steven walked back to the cabin and locked the door.

As he approached the car he could see Roy slumped in the passenger seat. He went to the driver's side, threw his backpack in the back seat, and turned to check on Roy.

"What are you doing back here?" Steven asked.

Roy didn't respond. His eyes were open, but unresponsive. There was a small trickle of blood coming from his nose. Steven shook him, but Roy didn't respond. He felt for a pulse – there was one. Roy was breathing.

"I've gotta get you out of here," Steven said, starting the car, and turning it around. He raced the car back down the dirt road. After a few minutes he reached the main highway and cell reception returned to his phone. He dialed 911.

"My father has had some kind of stroke," he said to the operator, "and I'm out in the middle of nowhere, on Highway 97, twenty miles south of Leavenworth. Where's the closest hospital?"

"No stroke," Roy said. "No hospital."

As the operator asked him more questions, Steven turned to Roy. "What? Dad, you were catatonic. You're bleeding."

"I'm fine. No hospital," Roy said, seeming to come back to life with each passing second.

"What do you mean you're fine?" Steven asked, ignoring the operator on the other end of his call.

"I mean," Roy said, wiping the blood from his nose, "I feel just fine."

"I wish I knew if I believed you," Steven said. "You didn't look very fine. Hold on a moment, operator," he said into the phone.

"I felt I was going to fall asleep, so I put myself into a trance. Sort of a defensive posture. I'm out of it now. I don't need a hospital."

Steven turned to the operator again, "I'm sorry, false alarm – he's OK." The operator started to object but Steven hung up on her.

"If you can protect yourself with a trance, why haven't you been doing that all along?" he asked Roy.

"Well, as you can see," Roy said, wiping the rest of the blood from his nose, "it comes at a price. I only did it because I was desperate. I didn't know how much longer you'd be, and I was starting to drift off lying in the cabin. I figured I'd walk back to the car to try and stay awake, and to be further from it, hoping it'd help. Seems to have worked."

"I'm sorry I took so long," Steven said. "I should have retuned sooner. I got caught up once I found the cave."

"Cave?" asked Roy.

"Yeah, another fifteen minutes past where you stopped," Steven told him. "I went a ways into it, didn't find a grave before I decided to turn around and come back."

"Did you go to the end of the cave?" Roy asked.

"No, it went on past where I stopped. When I ran into animal bones I thought it might make more sense to explore it armed."

"Good thinking," Roy said. "We'll use my Benelli."

"We're," Steven replied, "not going to use anything. I'll be using it. You can't go back there."

"If I have my protection, I'll be fine," Roy said.

"Forgive me if I doubt that," Steven replied.

"Look, you need me to find the grave in that cave," Roy said. "I can locate it."

"Locate it?" Steven asked. "How are you going to do that? You can't even get within a thousand feet of it, let alone locate it."

"That's because I didn't have my protection," Roy said. "Look, you need to trust me on this. I know what I'm doing. I've been doing it a long time."

"You're telling me if you drink that stuff, you'll be able to walk into that cave without a problem? After what we saw today, you'll be able to just walk along, carrying a shotgun, and help me survey a dark cave, full of water?

"Yes."

"And not fall and break something, not get sick?"

"Yes."

"I don't want to have to carry you out of there."

"You won't have to."

"How do I know?" Steven raised his voice, angry and frustrated. "How do I know that? If you collapse in that cave and I have to carry you out, I'm not sure I can do that."

Roy didn't respond. A moment of uncomfortable silence passed. Steven remembered the fear he felt as he left the cave earlier that morning. He couldn't imagine trying to do that with his father slung over his shoulder.

"Listen," Roy said calmly. "I realize you think I'm an old geezer who is two steps away from falling into my own grave. And I realize you think my protection is bogus, and I'm too weak to defend myself. You think everything is worse than it is, you always have. You don't understand these things, they're all a mystery to you, you're frightened because of your perspective."

"No, that's not it," Steven said. "It has nothing to do with my perspective."

"Then what?" Roy asked. "Why do you think I can't handle myself?"

Steven felt tears surfacing, and he fought to stop them from appearing in front of his dad. "Because I'm worried you'll get hurt. That you'll misjudge something and be permanently hurt. Or worse, that I might lose you. And I don't want that to happen."

Roy reached across the seat and placed his hand on Steven's shoulder. Steven couldn't remember the last time his dad had touched him this way.

"I'm more worried about you, kiddo," Roy said.

Eighteen

They agreed on the way home that they would not return to the cave until the next day, when they'd have plenty of daylight to maneuver in the woods. They stopped for food and then returned to Roy's house, the sky already starting to darken. Roy went about gathering the various guns he thought they should use, and ammo, and placed them on the kitchen table.

"You could outfit the army of a small country," Steven said, looking over the pile.

"We can decide later which ones we want to take," Roy said. "I'm going to be in my bedroom for a while."

"Not sleeping, I hope," Steven said.

"No, not sleeping. Making more of this," Roy said, shaking the empty Mason jar.

"Can I watch?" Steven asked.

"I'd rather you didn't," Roy said.

"Why?"

"It'll just make me fuck it up. I've always made it by myself, if you watch I'll get something wrong."

"Nothing like confidence in the family," Steven said.

"I have enough confidence to know you need to stay the hell out while I make it. I want to be able to concentrate and make a strong batch."

"How long? I'm going to check on you if it goes past the time you tell me."

"Half an hour," Roy replied, and walked back to the bedroom.

Steven was intrigued by whatever was going on behind his father's bedroom door. He could hear rustling, and once he thought he heard chanting. He was careful not to make any noise; he didn't want to disturb Roy in any way, make him think he'd been distracted. *Even if the stuff is just psychosomatic, it works for the guy, and he needs it,* he thought. Anything that might help, he was for.

Steven noticed the book on the kitchen table under the guns, the secret book his father had tossed there a day before. He had told him to look through it, to see if he could find anything that might help. He pulled it out and flipped through it.

The book was both old and new. It was bound, but handmade, and had been expanded and reinforced several times. All of the writing was by hand, with some drawings. As he flipped through it he noticed that the writing became more modern as he progressed. At the end he noticed it was his father's handwriting.

He returned to the front of the book and looked for changes. There were four sections where the style of writing and the paper incorporated into the book changed significantly. Steven realized this book had been given to Roy, and Roy was updating it with his own experiences and knowledge. *This section just before Roy,* Steven thought, *was this the writing of Roy's father? Has this been in the family for generations?*

He flipped back through the center of the book, tried to read the writing. It was difficult. The words were in English, but the meaning seemed to rely on something else not contained within the text, like a key or some bit of knowledge that Steven didn't have. Some sections looked like lists, or recipes, but he couldn't determine what they would make or what they were for. There were occasional drawings. He didn't know how long he had been turning the pages when he came across one drawing that made his blood run cold. It was the head of a man, with no eyes. Curling out of the back of the head were horns, like those of a goat. The lower half of the image was charred and burned. He ran his fingers over it, and carbon came off on them.

"That was where your mother tried to burn it," Roy said, behind him. "That was something your great-grandfather dealt with, and his drawing of it scared her."

"What was it?" Steven asked.

"Some kind of demon," Roy said. "Would have been about 1890. He lived in California."

"What happened?"

"Don't know. Your mother burned up most of the page where he wrote about it. Hope we never run into one, we'll have no idea what to do."

"I'm guessing the fact that the book is still intact means you rescued it from her?"

"Yes," said Roy. "She could barely stand the idea of me being involved with any of this. But when she saw that drawing, it flipped her Jesus switch big time. I stopped her from destroying it but she insisted I hide it away and make sure you kids never saw it. Told me if she ever saw me reading it again, she'd divorce me. And I knew she meant it. Your mother didn't make idle threats."

Steven shook his head in agreement. "So this book is the reason I had to sit through church all those years?" he asked.

"Yes, I'm afraid so," Roy said. "She's probably pissed you're seeing it now."

"How far back does this go?" Steven asked.

"Four generations," Roy replied. "Your great, great grandfather Thomas is first. Then his son, Charles, my grandfather. Then my father, David. Then me."

"This is incredible," Steven said. "I thought when you said a secret book you meant some kind of…well, I don't know, I don't know exactly what I thought. But I didn't think this. This is a family history. This is valuable."

"You think so?" Roy asked. "I'm glad to hear you say that. Because when I die, I'm not leaving it to Bernie."

Steven looked at Roy. "Well," Steven stammered, "I'd be honored to have it. Really, Dad. I'm sure I can take care of it, maybe have it protected so it doesn't deteriorate," he said, turning the pages. "Some parts of this are so old, I'm worried they'll become brittle."

"You do that. In the meantime, it's mine," Roy said, taking it out of Steven's hands. "I'm not finished with it."

"Of course," Steven said.

"Potion's done, made it extra potent. Time to work on a way to dispense of Mr. Johansen. You sleep first. I need to start going through this in detail, looking for something that will head us in the right direction."

Steven retreated to the guest bedroom and tried to go to sleep. He could hear his father turning pages in the other room, studying the book. He wondered what Roy would write about their current problem in the book, after it was finished. He wondered if Roy had memorized the look of Lukas' image in the trance, so he could draw it in the book like his predecessors. He realized more was going on with Roy than it appeared. *He's a tough old man,* Steven thought. *Tougher than I thought.*

He drifted off to sleep.

◊

Roy woke Steven around 4 a.m.

"Any luck?" Steven asked.

"No," Roy said. "My eyes are tired from all the reading, I'm seeing nothing but blurs."

"Sleep," Steven said. "I'll wake you at nine."

Roy padded off to his bedroom, and Steven poured himself a cup of coffee from the pot Roy had made during his stint. He sat at the kitchen table and stretched his eyes open, trying to clear the sleep from them. The book lay open where Roy had left it, and Steven tried to focus on the page. He decided to wait until after the coffee had done its job. He walked into the bathroom, intending to take a piss and splash some water over his face. As he flushed the toilet and moved to the sink, he noticed the sink was full of water. The stopper was up, but the sink was full.

He turned to look at the bathtub. Also full. *It's here,* he thought.

He left the bathroom and walked down the short hallway to his father's bedroom. The door was open a crack. He knew it was there before he could see inside. As he pushed the door open, the shadow came into full view against the far wall. The image was constantly shifting, as though it was obscured by moving glass. Roy was not in his bed, but suspended in the air near the ceiling between Steven and the shadow. Roy's body was shaking in the same manner Steven remembered from their last encounter.

Fearful that his father would fall to the floor, he ran to the center of the room and stood under him, ready to catch him. He then faced the shadow, intending to dispel it as he had learned.

Something made him stop short of shouting the banishment. Once he positioned himself under Roy he felt the same ice-cold blade he had felt at the third encounter with the shadow. It sliced though his torso, but this time there was no pain, just shock. He felt the blade inside him, twisting, but he felt no need to run. He just stood there and waited for what might happen next. He saw his father's body shaking above him, and he knew he didn't have much time for experimentation. But something told him to wait and see what would happen.

He felt the blade rise inside him. As it entered his head, the room was suddenly too bright to bear. Dark images were now white, and white images were a series of greys. Everything had been thrown into negative.

I'm being attacked now, Steven thought.

Correct, he heard Roy think. His father was still suspended above him, but he knew the message was coming from Roy.

What do I do? he thought.

See if you can talk to it, he heard.

Talk to it? To the shadow?

Yes, he heard. *I can't. See if you can learn something about it we could use against it.*

Steven turned his attention to the shadow. The eyes were still there, looking at him. He sensed awareness behind them, and he tried to communicate with it, but nothing seemed to work. He thought sentences: "Who are you?" "What are you?" "What do you want?" but got nothing in return except the continued staring.

Anything? he heard from Roy.

No. Nothing.

Try another way, he heard.

Steven considered what this meant, and closed his eyes. Immediately his mind was filled with a rushing torrent of motion, flowing from his father down into him and then on to the shadow, which now looked more like a man. *This is the draining*, he thought. *The shadow forces the flow to him from us.* Steven pictured going inside the flow, as though he was riding an inner tube through a waterslide tunnel in an amusement park.

That worked. The shadow was now the creature he had seen in the hallway, grotesque and threatening. In a moment, he was at the creature from inside the flow. He was stopped from getting close to it by the panes of glass, shifting and distorting the image beyond, which appeared in pain. He strained to see more, but the shifting glass caused him to lose focus and he couldn't concentrate on any one thing long enough to figure it out. The image beyond was moving its lips, but the distortion kept him from making out what it was saying. He felt his lungs collapsing, as though he had held his breath for too long, and felt as though he might pass out. He waited as long as he could, gasping for air, before he decided he could bear no more.

Steven opened his eyes and thought, "Be gone!"

In an instant, the room changed back to its former light, the shadow began to recede, and he felt his father fall on top of him. Steven broke the fall with his own body, and the two lay in a heap in the middle of the room.

"Help me up," Roy said. "I gotta know what happened." He was pushing himself off Steven, who struggled to his knees.

"Ow," Steven grimaced, holding his head. "Oh, damn, that hurts."

"I don't weigh that much," Roy complained.

"It's not you," Steven said, holding the side of his head and furrowing his brow. "It feels like someone is jamming an icepick in my brain."

"Oh, that," said Roy. "You'll get used to it. I suppose now I should get *you* some aspirin."

"Yes, please, this is fucking unbearable," Steven said.

Roy got to his feet and led Steven out of the bedroom and back to the kitchen table. After sitting him down, he rounded up the medicine and gave it to Steven, who downed it quickly.

"It'll go away after a few minutes," Roy said. "Jumping in can fuck up your head for a while. Especially when it's your first time in charge, which I'm guessing that was."

"Son of a bitch!" Steven cried, holding his head between his knees. "This really hurts. I think I'm gonna be sick." He raised his head and raced for the bathroom. Roy could hear him retching for the next several minutes. He took the time to make a new pot of coffee.

Steven emerged from the bathroom and stood at the kitchen entrance, staring at Roy.

"Feel better now?" asked Roy.

"Yeah," Steven replied, "I do. It still hurts, but not like they're slicing my head open with a cleaver anymore."

"I remember my first time," Roy said, smiling, pouring a cup of coffee for Steven. "Nineteen sixty-two, in Arizona. Had an interesting experience with a Thunderbird. And I don't mean a car or booze." He handed the cup to Steven, who took it.

Steven sat at the table, sipping the coffee, coming down from the pain. He saw the book on the table and noticed the page it was turned to. He glanced over it, but was surprised to find that a couple of the words made sense. Not all of it, but some of it, here and there. The more he read the clearer it became.

"You were reading this when I took over for you?" Steven asked, pointing at the page.

"Yes," answered Roy.

"This section here? This part? 'Invitations'?" Steven asked.

Roy smiled broadly, surprised. "Yes, that very part!"

"You set that up, didn't you?" Steven asked. "You read about this in your book while I was sleeping, and you woke me up just to see if this would work, right? That's why the attack started moments after you went to bed. That wasn't a normal attack from you falling asleep, like before. You made it happen. You invited him."

"Yes!" Roy said enthusiastically. "Now, tell me what you learned."

"Wait just a minute," said Steven. "I want to make sure I understand what just happened here. You put yourself into a trance that you knew would draw the shadow. Something you read about."

"Yes," replied Roy, "and he showed up almost immediately. The guy is following us everywhere we go, waiting for any opportunity. He's hungrier than a cranky bear after hibernation."

"And you banked on me coming to save you," Steven said.

"Yes," said Roy. "And this trance I used, it was different. It made it easier for him to get at me, but it also made it easier for you to join and take control."

"That's why you were floating near the ceiling instead of an inch off the bed," Steven said.

"Was I?" Roy asked. "That's right, I fell on you, so I must have been above you. Anyway, you did jump in. That's what matters."

"My point is," Steven said, "what if I hadn't? How much faster was he draining you?"

"Much faster," said Roy. "I doubt I'd have lasted ten minutes."

"It was a dumb move. I don't understand why you couldn't tell me you were going to try this before you did it. Why leave my involvement to chance?"

"Because," said Roy, "it's like telling a scared kid he's going to have to jump into the swimming pool when he doesn't want to, versus giving him a reason to jump in. A little push, if you will. And you jumped. It worked."

"Only because I thought you were in danger."

"If that was true," said Roy, "you would have banished it as soon as you came in the room. Instead, you chose to jump into the river and check things out. And you found out you can swim. Now tell me what you found out."

Steven relayed, as best as he could describe in words, the experience of the flow and his watertube, the glass wall and the images behind the glass.

"That's Lukas, behind the glass," Roy said. "Did you hear anything?"

"His lips moved," Steven replied, "but I couldn't hear what he was saying. It was just…sounds."

"The glass," asked Roy, "was it hard? Did you touch it?"

"It stopped me," said Steven. "But it wasn't solid. It was moving, making it hard to see."

"Moving like what? Back and forth? Wavy, like water?"

Steven thought about this. Yes, it was a lot like water. And once he realized it was water, the sounds he had heard began to organize in his mind.

"Yes, water," he told Roy. "Water makes sense. And the sounds he made sounded like they were coming from under water. That's not normal when you're in a trance?"

"Very little is normal," answered Roy. "Each can be different. You're learning to work with a new vocabulary, a new system of thinking. Each experience you have will teach you to put things into context, and that will clarify other things that didn't make sense before. Like the book. You can read some of it now, can't you."

"Yes," Steven answered, "the section on invitations at least."

"Whereas before," Roy continued, "the words didn't make sense to you at all."

"Right," Steven answered.

"Now that you know he was under water, think back to the sounds again. What did he say?"

Steven thought. The sounds were there in his mind, still a jumble of individual noises. He imagined the water and the image of the man behind it, the lips moving. The sounds began to clarify in his mind and come together.

"He said, 'can't breathe.'"

"Ha ha!" Roy said, slapping the kitchen table. "That's why he's weak! That's why he can't summon Michael to finish the deed!"

Steven wasn't sure he fully understood what Roy was saying, but Roy seemed to know where he was going with it.

"The cave," Roy asked, "had water in it?"

"A stream running through it. There were several pools in the rooms I saw at the end – or, where I stopped."

"How deep?"

"Maybe a couple of inches. Maybe more, I don't know, I didn't check them out."

"Ben buried him in the cave," said Roy, "but the water in the cave changed, covering the body. That's why Lukas is so weak. He needs a connection before he can latch onto someone. The only connection he could make was through that house, where he had success draining Ben. He couldn't waste his energy just randomly trying to connect to someone; the water kept him weak, made it hard for him to connect, and he couldn't afford to waste what he'd drained from Ben. Ben's journal, under the floorboards, was a perfect focal point for him. Once we came into proximity with the journal, he latched onto us. "

"Onto you, you mean," Steven corrected.

"Onto us. You've been part of it from the beginning. And once he started draining us, he's raised enough energy to follow us around, so he could drain more whenever possible."

"But he has been draining you, not me," Steven said. "The attacks have been on you."

"You don't feel anything?" Roy asked.

"I still feel the headache," Steven said.

"That's the river," Roy replied. "That's normal, that's not it. Don't you feel exhausted?"

"That's because we've had damn little sleep," Steven said.

"You think," Roy said, "that when you watch over me while I'm sleeping, it's to avoid an attack, but when I watch over you, it's just to make sure you get some shuteye?"

Steven considered this. He did feel exhausted, both mentally and physically. Sleep had been hard to come by. But he also felt something else missing, a piece of him that was much smaller than it used to be. He didn't think he would have noticed it before today, or have known how to identify it. But now he could tell it was missing. The same way the experience in the river had made him able to read some of the book, and understand some of the words, he was able to assess himself and realize he was being drained.

"It was attacking me before I even came to you," Steven said.

"I could tell the day you showed up, asking for that next of kin thing. You had no idea. That's why I got involved."

Steven swallowed hard. He knew what his father was saying was true. He had slept through it all, but his father had recognized it. His dad seemed know what he was doing.

"Why didn't you tell me?" Steven asked.

"You wouldn't have believed me, you never do. Some things you just have to figure out as you go."

"And this stunt tonight," Steven said, "was about doubling our forces."

"I think we're both finally on the same page. What I'm afraid of now is that he's drained enough power from the two of us to contact Michael."

"To finish the ritual?" Steven asked.

"Exactly. Michael doesn't know where Lukas is buried any more than we do – but he will wait in the wings until we release him. My guess is, after tonight, he'll be following us."

"Then how do we stop it? Anything in there," Steven motioned to the book, "that will stop it?"

"From what I've been reading, our best chance is to burn him. Incinerate the body. Fire is a cleanse, it gets rid of everything."

Steven sighed. "If the body is in a grave under water, provided we can find it and dig him up, it'll be soaked."

"Maybe not," said Roy, "if Ben put him in a box first."

"A waterproof box? I think you're giving Ben too much credit."

"Maybe you're right," said Roy.

"In any event, we can't risk removing the water," Steven said. "According to you, that's what's keeping him weak. It makes no sense to remove it and give him any kind of an opportunity. If there was some way we could keep him under water, and transport the body out to Puget Sound, we could just weigh him down and dump him."

"I'm not sure that would end it," Roy said. "Water is water. I'm not so sure that a hundred feet will matter more than a couple of inches."

"He'd be fish food," Steven said. "Eventually the body would be gone."

"If that were true, he'd be gone already from insects. The problem is he's not completely dead, not even now, not after fifteen years in the ground. The body needs to be gone, completely, if we want to stop the attacks."

"So we've got to burn it," Steven said.

"Yes."

"While it's under water."

"Yes."

"What burns under water?"

They both thought for a moment.

"Flares," Roy said, smiling. "I have a box in the basement." He jumped up and walked to the basement stairs. "I'll be right back," he said, disappearing down them.

Steven removed his phone and searched for "burn under water." Sure enough, he found a YouTube video showing a flare burning in a bucket of water. The description of the video said it was an ordinary roadside flare. He heard Roy rummaging around, then coming back up the stairs.

Roy placed a large cardboard box on the floor between them. The side of the container said "144 count."

"Why would you need a whole case of flares?" Steven asked.

"They were on sale at Costco," Roy replied. "Great price. I was gonna give some of them to you and Bernie but never got around to it. Forgot they were down there."

"How old are they?" Steven said, removing one and examining it.

"Couple of years," Roy replied, grabbing a flare himself. "Maybe seven or eight years. Let's test one."

Roy took the flare to the bathroom and began filling the tub. Steven followed him, trying to read the instructions that were printed on the side of the flare, but the lettering was too small to make out. Once several inches accumulated, Roy removed the plastic cap from the end of the flare and struck it against the tip. After a couple of attempts, it came to life, sputtering and dripping molten material into the bathtub.

"Ready?" Roy asked.

"Yes," Steven replied. Roy sunk his hand into the tub, immersing the flare. It did not stop burning. Water bubbled up around Roy's hand. He held it under the water for over a minute, then let it sink to the bottom of the tub, where it continued to burn.

"How long will it go for?" Steven asked.

"Ten, fifteen minutes," Roy replied. "Maybe more."

"One of these won't be enough to incinerate a body."

"But a dozen would do some damage," Roy said.

"How are we going to work that?" Steven asked.

"We bundle a bunch of them together," Roy explained, "like sticks of dynamite. All with the burning edge facing the same direction. We'll have to remove the dirt that's covering him while leaving the water in place. We light them all at the same time with a blowtorch, then we place the burning side down through the water and into the body. We should make several of them, so we can hit him with dozens of them all at once. We could each hold two bundles, one in each hand. We'd be hitting him with almost fifty of them, all at once. And they'll burn for a while. That's got to do a lot of damage. Maybe enough that after they run out, we can remove the body safely from the water and incinerate what's left with the blowtorch."

"This is insane," Steven said.

"Yeah, but I think it will work," Roy said.

"It might. How do we bundle them?"

Roy set about gathering the remaining items they'd need to construct and prepare the flares. He duct-taped a dozen of them together, and then used the duct tape to make a handle on the bottom of the bundle. Then he returned with the blowtorch.

"Should we test it?" Roy asked.

"Yes," Steven said. "I'd rather not have any surprises. We need something like a big chunk of meat."

"How about a roast?" Roy offered. He went to the refrigerator and removed a chuck roast, about an inch thick and ten inches in diameter.

"Why not?" Steven said. They took the roast to the bathtub. Roy unwrapped it, and dropped it in.

"You hold the flares," Roy said. "I'll light it with the blowtorch. Once they're all going, use the handle to press it down into the water and into the roast."

Roy snapped the blowtorch to life and Steven held it over the tub, pointed away from both of them. Once all twelve were lit, it was extremely bright and Steven had to squint to see what he was doing. The heat coming from it and the vibration caused by the group of burning flares made him feel like he was carrying a lethal weapon. He sank it into the water, and immediately the water began to erupt around him in response. He kept pressing it downward until he felt it hit the roast. Then he held it there.

Steven and Roy looked at each other.

"This will work," Roy told him. "I'm sure."

"How long do I hold it here?" Steven asked.

"Until they burn out," Roy replied. "When we're doing this for real, each of us will have two of them, one in each hand, and we'll be pressing them all down into Lukas's body. We want every bit of these flares to burn up as much of the body as possible. We don't stop until there's no body left, or until the flares give out."

The aroma bubbling up from the bottom of the tub was appetizing, not unlike the smell of a roast cooking on the stove.

"Making me hungry!" Roy said.

The process took a while. "Isn't he going to fight back while we're doing this?" Steven asked Roy.

"I don't think so," Roy replied. "His body is still inert. It's his mind that's active."

"Fight us with his mind, then."

"Maybe. That's why we'll dose up on protection before we go."

Steven thought about this, unsure he wanted to drink Roy's concoction. Still, it made sense to take every precaution. Steven felt himself giving in to Roy. Roy was winning him over.

The first of the flares exhausted themselves after ten minutes and after another couple of minutes the last finished. They pulled the flares from the tub and looked in for the roast. There were only bits of charred meat floating around in the water, mixed with the material from the flares.

"That's good enough for me," Roy said. "How about you?"

"Let's finish the rest of them," Steven said.

Nineteen

Steven let Roy sleep as they drove back to the cabin. Roy had grabbed a few hours of sleep after they finished creating the weapons, and Steven had used the time to read through the book. He found a few parts that made sense to him. The words seemed out of order, but he could rearrange them in his mind and construct a meaning. Still, much of the book seemed impenetrable, nonsensical. He took Roy's word that those sections were areas he had no experience with. That was most of the book.

Of the parts he could read, he found them highly intriguing. Invitations, he learned, could be used for all kinds of purposes, usually to the advantage of the initiator, but not always. In the older section of the book he found several sections that spoke of transformation and metamorphosis, ways to transform and ways to stop it. There were also some sections that spoke generally about the river, how to enter and exit it with less pain, and how to maneuver within it. He found several areas that spoke of protection, but they were still jumbled to him. He made a note to come back and read about them after he downed Roy's potion and see if they cleared up.

The more he read, the more intrigued he became. He felt himself falling into something that he knew even a week ago he would have resisted with all his heart as ridiculous and superstitious. The connection to his father and his father's father was part of it, he supposed. This wasn't some reality show ghost story he could easily dismiss as superstition. This was something with a deliberate history, intended for him.

The parts written by Roy were the most baffling. It was as though his father was writing in an entirely different language, one Steven had never heard. His respect for Roy jumped significantly. He had accomplished many things Steven knew nothing about. And still didn't. But the writing was extensive, and part of Steven yearned to learn what it was, to take advantage of what his father had felt needed to be written.

After Roy awoke, they had loaded the flare bundles and the guns into backpacks in the trunk of Steven's car. They decided one of them would carry the 9mm and the other would carry a sawed off shotgun. Roy had pointed out to Steven how to operate each one, where the safeties were, how to load them.

Roy snored quietly as Steven piloted the car up Interstate 90, driving into the morning sun. *This was the last day,* he thought. *No more after today.* He envisioned his house in a normal state, returning to a normal pattern of life. *I can go back to...what was I doing?* he thought. He honestly couldn't remember what had occupied his days after he was let go, before the hauntings began. It made him a little melancholy.

He wondered where Ben was buried, how it had been for Ben in the final days, if he had tried to return to the grave site and correct his mistake. *Maybe, by the time he realized what was happening, he didn't have the strength,* Steven thought. *Ben at least had the good sense to haunt the place.* Steven wondered if any of the four owners of the house between Ben and himself had made it as far as Steven, if they had encountered the shadow, if it had drained them too. If any of them had pieced it together. If maybe he and Roy weren't the first to attempt what they were about to do.

After an hour, he turned onto the highway that led to the cabin. Another twenty minutes and they could turn onto the small road that was the final leg of the trip.

Steven felt nervous, but at the same time confident. He supposed he was picking up on Roy's confidence, that it was rubbing off on him. As Steven thought back over the past several days, he realized Roy had no fear. Roy had taken delight in confronting everything they had encountered. He didn't hesitate. Steven thought he had been reckless, failing to consider consequences. But through it all, Roy's approach had worked. Each time they had progressed, gaining new information they needed to tackle the problem. He knew Roy didn't know the outcomes before he jumped, but he jumped anyway. Steven presumed it was because of a character flaw, but now he saw that it was just courage.

Or experience. As far as Steven knew, Roy may have encountered far more frightening things than they were confronting now. Either way, Steven realized he'd been wrong. Roy was right, Steven didn't give him enough credit. He looked over at the sleeping man in the car, and his admiration grew. *He knew I'd figure this out,* he thought. *I need to trust him.*

As the car approached the spot in the road where they would stop and walk to the cabin, Steven woke Roy. "We're here," he said.

Steven reached for the door handle, but Roy stopped him. "Wait," he said. "Before we go out, this." He produced the Mason jar. He removed the lid and handed it to Steven. "Two large gulps. It'll sting, like booze."

Steven took the jar, looked at the clear liquid once more, and raised it to his lips. It went down more smoothly than he anticipated. He felt it spreading out inside him.

"Not bad. You must have used the good vodka," Steven said to Roy, handing it back.

"Nah, I find the rat shit smooths out the Popov," he replied, taking two large gulps for himself, capping the jar and returning it to the backpack at his feet.

"Rat shit?" Steven asked.

"Just fucking with ya," Roy said, getting out of the car.

By the time they dropped their gear in the cabin, Steven was feeling euphoric, with a tingling moving through his muscles.

"Wow," he said to Roy, stretching his arms and fingers. "That drink is something else. I'm surprised you're not addicted to it."

"Gives me the runs," Roy said. "And don't get cocky. You're not stronger. All it does it make it harder for others to mentally attack you. It impacts them, not you. So don't do anything stupid."

"Anything else we need to do before we go up to the cave?" Steven asked.

"I don't think so," Roy said. "We've gone over the guns, we've got the flares and blowtorch, and we're dosed up. I think that's it."

"Dad," Steven said, walking over to him. "If there's something you're planning you haven't told me about, please tell me now. I don't want you to take unnecessary risks. You don't need to. You don't need to surprise me with something new because you think I won't understand if you explained it beforehand. I'd rather be partnered with you, knowing what we're trying to do, than trying to catch up to you."

"You know everything I'm thinking," Roy said. "No surprises. We do it just like we've talked about it." Roy grabbed a backpack, slung it around his back. "But son, listen to me."

Steven stopped. Roy didn't often call him son.

"You have certain expectations of how thing work," Roy said. "You're used to doing things a certain way that's predictable. You like to plan things out and then have everything go to plan. Sometimes that works. Sometimes it doesn't work."

"I know shit can happen," said Steven. "I just wanted to be sure you understood that you don't need to hide anything from me."

"That's not what I'm saying," Roy answered. "Sometimes the plan has to be trusting in your own ability to react. Sometimes a plan goes off rails so early, there was no point in the planning. What matters is your ability to make quick decisions, not get slowed down by seeing a plan unravel. Everything we've prepared for dealing with this sonofabitch might blow up in our faces. You've got to trust that you can still move forward, not freeze up or second-guess yourself. I know that's something you're not used to, but it's something I'm hoping you'll do."

Steven thought about this. Roy was right, he knew it. "I've been learning a lot from you, Dad," Steven said. "Far more than you realize. Far more than I've realized. It's just difficult to trust in something you can't see."

"Oh, if that's the only problem," replied Roy, "then just open your eyes. You'll see it."

Steven picked up his backpack. "I'll try, Dad. Let's go."

◊

As they stood at the entrance to the cave, Roy was becoming visibly agitated.

"Is something wrong?" Steven asked.

"No, nothing wrong," Roy replied. "It's just…he's in there."

"You're sure?"

"Ninety-nine percent."

"You're not feeling sick like before?"

"No," Roy replied, "just apprehensive. He'll be a cornered animal in there. Makes him more dangerous."

"I can tell this isn't the first time you've cornered something," Steven said.

"A creature in a mine shaft in Utah," Roy said. "Long before I met your mother. It knew its way around the mine a lot better than I did. That's why I'm a little concerned."

"At least we know this one is buried," Steven replied, feeling anxious himself.

Steven walked into the cave, Roy followed. Steven used a flashlight, Roy held a battery lantern that was designed to sit on the ground and light up an area.

Steven guessed they were about halfway to the first room in the tunnel when he stopped and turned to Roy to check in.

"Still doing OK?" he asked.

"Fine."

"Feeling anything?"

"The body's up ahead," Roy said. "It feels stronger."

Steven turned and continued down the path. After several minutes they emerged into the first small room.

"Not here," Roy said almost immediately. "Not enough water."

They progressed to the next small room, where Roy made the same pronouncement.

In the third room, the water was more substantial. Steven pointed out the animal bones to Roy. "They must be very old," Roy said. "There are no animals in here anymore. They wouldn't live this near it."

Steven took that to be a good thing – not running into any bears or bobcats took his stress level down a notch. He kept glancing at Roy, looking for signs that he might be tiring or becoming sick. If he was feeling worse, he was covering it well.

"What about the water, over there?" Steven asked.

"Not here," Roy replied. "Stronger up ahead. We're not there yet."

There were two passages leading out of this room; they chose the one that contained the stream of water.

The passageway was still tall enough to easily stand upright, and both Steven and Roy walked slowly and carefully through it, avoiding the water at their feet. After another hundred feet the passageway opened into a large room, much larger than the previous three. Steven guessed it was about fifty yards wide and the same length. The ceiling was high. Scanning the walls of the room, Steven saw some fissures but they were all small; a person would have to slide into them sideways to progress. There was no easy exit from the room other than the way they entered. The floor was a combination of dirt and rock, and located in the middle of the room was a large pond of water that reflected their bouncing lights. The water looked black and still.

"He's here," said Roy. "In there."

Steven suddenly wished they had brought more lights. In the smaller rooms a flashlight did an adequate job, but in this large room the light quickly dissipated. He felt an overwhelming desire to just flick a switch and have the place illuminate.

The pond was about forty feet across. Water ran out of it and down the passageway, forming the stream they had followed. He scanned the edge of it and could see no inlet. "The water must come from underneath," he said.

"And that's why the grave is probably near an edge," Roy replied. "I think Ben buried him next to it in dry ground, but then the lake expanded and covered the grave. This room has probably seen cycles of the water rising and falling throughout the years. Lucky for us it's been on a rising cycle for the past fifteen."

"Why don't we walk the perimeter a little, and see if you can pick up on where he's at," Steven said. Roy sat his lantern down and grabbed a camping shovel from his backpack.

The two of them paced around the edge of the pond, going slowly, shining their flashlight into the first three feet of water. Steven stopped and placed his hand into the water, about two feet out. It sunk only an inch.

"That's good." said Roy. "I'd hate to dig through a foot of water."

They continued walking around the perimeter. When they reached the point about halfway from the room's entrance to the back of the chamber, Steven felt a tug in his chest, and he stopped walking.

"You felt it," Roy said.

"Yeah, like something pulling inside me," Steven said.

Another step, and the feeling increased. Two more steps, and it subsided. Steven backtracked to the place where it had felt the strongest.

"Now," said Roy, "we just need to know how far into the water."

They both walked straight into the water, starting at the point where the tug was the strongest. After two steps they were standing in an inch of water. After another two, it came to their ankles.

"Too far," Steven said, taking a step backwards. "Here."

Roy stood next to him. "Yes, it's the strongest here. This is it." He took the shovel and stuck it through the water and into the ground as a marker.

"Damn, I wish we'd brought more light," Steven said.

"I need to move the lantern closer to this point on the shore," Roy said. "That will help some." He turned and walked out of the water towards the spot where they had left the lantern.

Steven remained at the shovel. The feeling in his chest was new and unusual, and a little disconcerting, because anything in your chest feels like it might be a heart attack. He lifted his feet and replaced them, trying to see what the ground under the water was like. It felt firm. He walked a little to the left and right, to see if the ground felt different after he stepped off the grave. It didn't. *Things have had plenty of time to settle,* he thought.

Roy returned with the lantern and now that it was only ten feet away things looked better, but he still wished they had stopped at a sporting goods store and invested in lights they could strap to their heads, like miners. Using a hand to hold a flashlight while out in the water began to seem like a disadvantage. Roy joined him.

"So what do you think is the best way to approach this?" Steven asked.

"Not sure," Roy answered. "I guess dig, and move each shovelful of dirt two or three feet away before you drop it back into the water, so it doesn't float back into where we're working."

"How will we know when we've reached him?" Steven asked.

"We'll have to use our hands," Roy replied.

A chill went up Steven's spine. It was creepy enough to be in the cave, let alone digging up a body. But to not be able to see it, and to have to feel into the dirt to know if you've reached it wasn't exactly how he imagined things playing out.

"Let's get started," Roy said, grabbing the shovel. He dug into the ground and pulled the shovelful up above the water level, where Steven shone the flashlight on it. The camping shovel was smaller than a regular shovel, collapsible, designed to easily fit into a backpack, and its blade was half the size of a normal shovel. It didn't bring up much, and what it did bring up looked like muck. Roy took a step to the side and dropped the muck back into the water. Then he took another shovelful and did the same thing. Steven saw the water around their feet become cloudy with the dirt they were stirring up.

After a dozen shovelfuls Roy bent over and sunk his hands into the hole he'd created underwater, to feel around.

"Anything?" Steven asked.

"Nothing."

"Here, let's trade off," Steven said. "You conserve your strength."

"I'm fine," Roy said, taking another shovelful. "I'm good for a few more inches."

Roy dug another dozen shovelfuls and dropped to his knees to check the depth again. He shook his head. "If Ben went six feet, this is going to be more challenging than I thought," he said.

"How deep are you now?" Steven asked.

"I'd say between six inches and a foot," Roy replied.

"It'll be in the next foot," Steven said confidently, fine tuning the sense he felt in his chest. Roy looked at him.

"You're sure?" Roy asked.

"Aren't you?" Steven replied.

Roy smiled at him. "That's my boy!" he said, digging another shovelful.

The next few minutes passed silently, Steven alternatively watching the spot where Roy was digging, and watching Roy for signs of weakness. Roy was breathing heavy, but not slowing. Twice he dropped to his knees and checked into the water with his hands.

Suddenly Roy stopped, holding the shovel but not proceeding. Roy had a concerned look on his face.

"What?" Steven asked.

"It's moving!"

"Under the water?"

"Under me, under my feet. I can feel movement!"

"Dad, get..."

But before Steven could finish warning Roy to move, he saw the hand emerge from the water, grasping at Roy. Roy jumped back and fell into the water.

"The shovel!" Steven shouted to Roy. "Use the shovel!"

The fingers on the hand were flexing, stretching, more testing their muscles than reaching for anything. The skin was stark white. Roy took the shovel and aimed it at the hand. He struck it with the blade, but it didn't cause any damage.

"Use the shotgun!" said Roy. Steven handed the flashlight to Roy, and Roy kept it on the hand while Steven swung his backpack off his back and in front of himself. He rummaged through it, retrieving the sawed-off shotgun. He swung the backpack around onto his back, and aimed the shotgun at the hand.

"No, no," Roy said. "Get right up next to it!"

Steven moved in closer, and placed the barrel of the shotgun about an inch away from the hand. He looked up at Roy, and Roy nodded approval. Then he pulled the trigger.

The sound reverberated inside the room and he heard the splashing of hundreds of pellets hitting the water. He was temporarily blinded by the flash from the gun. When he recovered his sight there was no hand above the water.

"Reach under there and see what we're dealing with," Roy said. "The bulk of him must still be under earth, or he'd be up by now."

"I thought you said the water was going to protect us," Steven said.

"Apparently it only dampens the mental side of it," Roy said. "It's not going to stop him from clawing his way out if he can."

"I wish you'd have brought that up when we were planning this," Steven said, becoming frustrated.

"We need to expose part of him, the head, the torso," Roy said. "Keep the extremities buried. Burn his core."

"Well, how the fuck are we going to do that, when we can't see what we're doing!" Steven said, exasperated.

Roy replied calmly. "Reach in and feel where things stand."

"Here," Steven said, handing Roy the shotgun. "Do not shoot me while I'm doing this."

Steven dropped to his knees next to where he remembered the hand emerging, and slowly slipped his fingers under the water. After moving them around a little, he found the stump of the arm. It moved when he touched it, bouncing back into his fingers, and he yanked his hand from the water in response.

"Found it," he said. "Took the hand off at the wrist. It's moving on its own."

"You gotta follow that arm down," Roy said, "and feel how much is exposed and how much is still buried."

"Fuck," Steven said. "Fuck, this is not how I thought this would go!"

"Like I told you," Roy replied. "Things don't always go as planned. No second guessing. Do it."

Steven reached under the water again, searching for the arm. He found it, and held it for a moment. There was no heat from the flesh, just the disturbing movement as the arm tried to wrestle free from his grip. He let it go and felt toward the elbow, which is where he ran into ground. He felt around, and could not locate the upper arm. "Only the part from the elbow on was out," he said to Roy.

"Good," Roy said. "What about around it? Anything else exposed?"

Steven widened his search a little. His fingers were beginning to get cold. He pressed them into rocks that felt like ridges.

"Might be ribs," he said.

He moved his hands further and found only dirt. The other side of the body was still covered. "The other arm is still underground," he told Roy.

"Move up," Roy said. "See if you can find his face."

Steven walked his fingers up from the ribs, and felt them slowly recede into the dirt. Then his fingers brushed the chin. He felt along the side of the head. His fingers were moving through less than an inch of dirt, and the movement of the water was removing much of what remained.

"The face is nearly exposed," Steven said.

"Good. Wait a second," Roy said, shifting his backpack. "Here, take the gun, will you?"

Steven removed his hands from the water, and Roy handed him the shotgun. Roy looked through his backpack, and removed a plastic baggie containing two thin rods. He handed the baggie to Steven, who took it.

"I want you to insert these into his eyes," Roy said.

"You've got to be kidding!" Steven said, looking at the contents. The two rods were actually wooden sticks, about three inches long. They were bent a little, like twigs from a tree. On each stick, one end had been roughly sharpened to a point with a knife.

"No, I'm not," Roy said. "Here, give me the gun back."

Steven handed Roy the shotgun and got back down on his knees. He removed a stick from the baggie and reached down into the water again, trying to locate the chin. He found it, then let his fingers move over the mouth and nose until he found an eye. Silt from the dirt still remained, but Steven could feel the eyelid opening and closing. It sent a chill down his back.

He took one of the sticks, and moved the sharp end down under the water, towards the eye. When he had it in position, he looked to Roy.

"Just shove it through?" he asked.

"Yup," Roy responded, "make sure it pierces the eye, not slip around it."

Steven closed his eyes, a move of self-preservation, and pushed. It slipped. He moved his other hand under the water to hold it in position, and pushed again. This time he felt it pierce through, and it sunk rapidly into the body. When it wouldn't go any further, he removed his hands. As he was preparing the second stick, he thought to himself, *this is smart. Even if he is able to free himself before we can finish, he'll be at a disadvantage.* He suspected Roy had additional reasons he wanted the sticks inserted, but this was good enough for Steven.

As he was lowering the second stick into position, he felt a larger movement, and the water began to shift. Wondering what was happening, he pulled back.

"No," Roy said. "Get the other eye. Quickly!"

Steven didn't have time. In front of him, the corpse rose, sitting up from its grave. Water poured from the body. Roy kept moving the light from Steven to the body, making it hard for Steven to see the body completely, but the shock of it caused him to fall back into the water, pushing himself away from the corpse.

All the features were intact, even the hair. As they both watched, the jaw opened, and the corpse seemed to suck in air. Then its undamaged arm reached up and removed the wooden stick from his left eye socket.

"The shotgun!" Steven yelled from his prone position. Roy stepped forward toward the body, raised the shotgun, and fired. The recoil took him off guard and he lost his footing under the water. He fell backwards, taking the flashlight and shotgun with him. Steven got to his feet, and recovered the flashlight, but the shotgun was somewhere under the water near Roy, who was on his back. He went to him and lifted him up. Roy was clearly in pain.

Steven shone the flashlight toward the body. The shotgun had taken away the other arm to the shoulder, but the torso and head remained. The corpse did not rise past a sitting position. *He's still buried below the legs,* Steven thought.

The remaining eye opened, and focused on Steven and Roy. Steven knew the eye instantly – same as the ones he'd encountered at his house in what seemed like an eternity ago. This was Lukas.

"Quick, the flares!" Roy said. Steven began removing them from his backpack, and Roy stuck the flashlight between his legs as he searched his backpack for the blowtorch.

They felt the air around them thicken. *Just like the hallway,* Steven thought. *This is the environment he works in. This is how he turns it to his advantage.*

Both Steven and Roy froze when they heard Lukas speak.

"You won't finish before I use you up," they heard. They both turned to Lukas, unsure if they had heard it in their minds, or if the corpse had actually spoken it.

Steven removed the first flare bundle from his backpack. "Light it!" he said to Roy. Roy had removed the blowtorch, and was clicking the igniter. He prayed it would ignite having been dampened when Roy fell in the water. It popped twice and then blew to life. Roy thrust the flame toward Steven, who held out the bundle for Roy to light.

Three-quarters of the flares were lit when Steven saw Roy move the flame away. He glanced up at him, and knew right away that something was wrong. His father was staring blankly to the side, his hand slowly lowering the flame. Then he dropped the blowtorch into the water completely, the flashlight fell from his knees, and he fell back into the water.

"Dad!" Steven screamed, and in an instant, he entered the flow between Roy and Lukas. He felt the cold knife enter him and slide up to his skull, much more quickly this time than last. He turned to look at Lukas. He was very much alive, looking strong and healthy despite the damage to his arm and hand. He had an amused look on his grotesque face, like he was enjoying what he was doing. *No doubt this is all about retribution now,* he thought. *We've ruined his body, his plans for eternal life are fucked. Now he just wants payback.*

Steven turned his vision back to Roy, who was arched on his back in the water, in pain. Lukas was draining Roy at an alarming rate. He could see there was little life left in him.

Steven knew he had to destroy Lukas immediately. He exited the flow, then moved toward Lukas with the flares, but again the atmosphere around him had thickened, and it was like trying to move through molasses. *Hold on, Dad,* he thought. He felt an overwhelming sense of desperation and hopelessness, that there was no point, that he should just give up.

"He's dead," said Lukas. "You should stop."

"You lie!" Steven replied, taking another step. He could sense Roy was still there, far away, still alive. But he wouldn't be for long. Steven forced his limbs to move, concentrating on each muscle.

"You're too weak," spoke Lukas again. "You won't make it. You should stop."

"I'm still coming," Steven said, and took another agonizingly slow step.

"I'm about to consume the last of your father. You'll never see him again. You should stop."

He forced his legs to move again. One more step and he'd be there. "Is this what you said to Ben?" he shouted at Lukas. "Is that how you terrorized him?"

"Every night I showed Ben how we tortured, killed and ate his son. We consumed his spirit and his soul. He watched it over and over. Soon your father will be dead, and I'll visit you every night. I'll show you how I sucked the life out of him, and how you let it happen! Soon you'll be cutting your eyes out too."

When he finally reached him he brought the flare bundle up to Lukas' face. Lukas moved backward defensively, towards the water. Steven followed him with the flares, moving in an agonizingly slow motion arc. When Lukas' head slipped below the surface he felt the thickness in the air evaporate. With all of his might he used both hands to shove the bundle down into the water and into the flesh of Lukas' face.

The water erupted with bubbles and the spit from the flares. The smell nauseated him as the flesh from Lukas' face was burned from his skull. *The flow is still occurring,* he thought. *He's still draining Roy. I have to speed this up.*

He let go of the bundle with his right hand, using the left to keep it firmly pressed against Lukas's head. With his free hand he removed another flare bundle from his backpack.

The blowtorch was too far away, and under water somewhere. *How am I going to light it?* He wondered, feeling panic and frustration well up inside him. *Improvise. Don't second guess.*

He pulled the burning flares from the water. They were still sputtering brightly. He could still feel Lukas' body shifting under him. He used the burning flares to light the new bundle, like a chain smoker. Then he returned the first bundle to Lukas' face and pressed the new bundle into his chest.

Lukas' body reacted strongly to the new flares and Steven felt pressure back, pushing him upward. But the more Lukas pressed to be free of the burning flares, the more Steven held them firm. Steven looked over his shoulder at Roy. He was prone in the water, on his back. His face was just above the water's surface. There wasn't enough light to see if he was still breathing.

He pressed harder on the bundles, feeling them make progress into the burning flesh below. *Burn, you motherfucker, burn!* he thought.

Then, as though Lukas had given up, he felt the resistance from the body below him stop, and he sensed the flow between Lukas and Roy drop. He resisted the urge to drop the flares and go check on Roy. Instead, he held the bundles in place, moving them slightly towards other unburned parts of Lukas' body.

Please be OK, he thought. He hoped he'd finished off Lukas before Roy was gone, but he had no way of knowing. He held the flares as they continued to burn in the water. As the first ones started to sputter out, he decided it was enough. He pulled the flares from the body, and dropped the bundles in the water next to him. Then he reached down to the corpse, and bent it upward, sitting it back up.

Most of the hair and flesh from the head was gone. In the torso, two large holes had burned through most of the body. The shoulders and arms were still intact. He couldn't see anything below the waist, where the body was still covered by water.

It wasn't moving, and Steven sensed no life – of any kind – in it.

He stood and walked over to Roy, calling to him. Roy was unresponsive. He reached for Roy's neck and felt for a pulse.

It was there, but it was very weak.

He tried to lift his father's body, and was able to drag him to the dry area of the cave, near the lantern. He observed him for a few moments. He was breathing, but very shallowly. He needed to get Roy out of the cave and to a hospital.

He walked back into the water and retrieved the shovel. They were not finished with their plan, which called for removing the body from the water, dousing it with lighter fluid, and burning off all remaining flesh, then reburying the bones. But Steven decided it was enough for now. Lukas was dead, and if not dead, he was too damaged to move. It was more important now to get help for Roy. He could return and finish later.

Steven consolidated the contents of the backpacks into one, slung Roy over his shoulder, grabbed the lantern, and walked out of the cave.

Twenty

"The doctors tell me they have to administer all your drugs intravenously because you won't swallow any pills."

"Goddamn right," Roy said. "Since when in this country do you have to swallow something you don't want to?"

Roy sat upright in his hospital bed, nervously fidgeting with the TV remote control.

"Doesn't matter that the drugs probably saved your life?" Steven asked.

"I know who saved my life," Roy said, looking at Steven. Steven looked down, embarrassed to look back at Roy.

"I'm glad you're finally awake," Steven said.

"How long was I out?"

"Three days," Steven replied. "And you slipped into a coma twice. The doctors didn't think you would make it after the second coma."

"Shows you what they know," Roy said. "Am I alone in this room? Any other people in here?"

"It's a private room," Steven said.

"Good," Roy said. "Then tell me about Lukas."

"What's the last thing you remember?" Steven asked.

"I remember lighting the flares you were holding," he answered. "Then nothing until here."

Steven retold the story to Roy, up to the point where he brought Roy to the hospital.

"And then you went back?" Roy asked.

"Yes, once you were situated here, I drove back. Went to the cave, intending to dig the rest of the body out, and burn what was left."

"It was gone," said Roy.

"How'd you know?" Steven asked.

"Didn't, it was a guess."

They both sat in silence for a moment.

"So," Steven sighed, "I cleaned everything up. There wasn't much to do. I took the cabin keys back to John and Debra. John asked me if I had been successful. I told him I thought so."

More silence.

"What do you think?" Steven asked. "Were we successful?"

"Well," Roy said, "I don't think Lukas got up and walked out. Not without a head or most of his torso."

"Everything is back to normal at the house," Steven said. "I slept there the last three nights, and no nightmares, no visions, no Ben. As far as I can tell, no Lukas either. I don't feel anything there, I don't feel like I'm being drained. I think he's gone."

"You're probably right," Roy said.

"Either that," Steven said, "or he's so severely damaged that he can't make the connection anymore."

"No, you're right," Roy said, "there's no connection. I could feel it constantly before. I don't feel it at all now."

"Might be the drugs," Steven said.

"That's why I don't like them!"

More silence. Steven paced around the base of Roy's hospital bed.

"There is one other possibility," Roy said.

"Yes?"

"Michael."

Steven looked at Roy. "Michael? What, he dug up the body? How did he know where it was?"

"He followed us," Roy said. "I felt he's been watching us ever since we confronted him, waiting to be there whenever we would eventually find Lukas."

"You think he went into the cave after I hauled you out," Steven asked, "and took Lukas's body?"

"Maybe."

"But Lukas was dead, it was over for Michael's plans. Why not just abandon the body?"

"Two reasons I can think of," Roy answered. "It could be that he's able to do something with what remains of Lukas."

"Regenerate him?"

"No, that's not going to happen. He might feel that the body still has some power, for some other purpose. It might act as an ingredient in some other recipe."

Steven hadn't considered this; there was so much about Roy's world he didn't know. "What, continue the transformation? Michael complete the ritual himself?"

"No, he can't do that," Roy said. "Michael is human, he doesn't have the DNA Lukas had. It could be some other process, to reclaim some of the power left in Lukas's body. That, or the other possibility, he just wished to honor the remains. Fifteen years of waiting, he was obviously attached to the guy. He might have just wanted to give Lukas a better resting spot than the watery grave Ben arranged."

Steven considered this. "Do we hunt down Michael?" he asked Roy.

"Why? If the hauntings and the draining have stopped, it's over."

"But," Steven protested, "four young kids were killed. He was involved."

"True," Roy said. "What do you propose?"

"We could go to the cops."

"Let me tell you something," Roy said. "In our line of work, you never go to the cops. Never, unless what you're taking to them meets their idea of how things work, and you're sure of how they'll handle it, based on their rules, not yours. Otherwise, they will peg you as a lunatic and you'll never be able to use them when you need them. Remember that. In this case, what would you do, tell them Michael kidnapped those kids?"

"Yeah," Steven said, "but you're right, I have no evidence."

"Exactly," Roy said, "you have to think like they think. It would be your word against his. And when the cops start asking why you've targeted him with these accusations, you won't be able to tell them how we found out without coming off like a crazy, unless you make something up, and then they will catch you in the lie. Trust me, I know how this works. Only deal with the cops when you're sure how they will react."

"We could take Michael on ourselves," Steven said.

"Why?"

"Because he killed those kids," Steven said, "and he has to pay. Because he's pissed that we killed Lukas, destroyed his grand plan, and he'll come after us for revenge. Because he's a bad man and needs to be removed from society, and if the cops won't do it, someone needs to. Are those reasons enough?"

"You're forgetting how he caused my gun to jam," Roy said. "Are you prepared to deal with that?"

"Doesn't your book have a death spell or something? Something we could use on him surreptitiously?"

"No, it doesn't," Roy answered. "Nothing like that. I don't see why we need to pursue Michael. All your reasons are fine, they're good reasons. But I don't think he's coming after us. And there are more threats to society than you and I can do anything about. Sometimes things don't wrap up cleanly, like in a movie. I keep trying to tell you this, you have to go with what happens. It's over, we did what we needed to do. You can go back to living a normal life, your house will leave you alone. I can sleep at night without the fear of being drained. We're good. Accept the fact that you won."

"It seems like a loose end," Steven said. "Like a dangerous loose end."

"I've got a lot of those," Roy said. "All over. It's not always a clean victory. Most of these situations wind up with some kind of stalemate. If Michael decides to come after us, then we can deal with him. But for now let the sleeping dog lie."

◊

Once he was awake, Roy recovered rapidly, and Steven drove him home from the hospital in a couple of days. Roy bitched about the hospital in the car all the way home. He seemed to be able to move around and function normally, and Steven developed some comfort watching him walk around his home as though nothing had happened. Apparently once the batteries were recharged, Roy was right back to normal.

Steven sat at the kitchen table while Roy puttered around the house arranging things. The book was still there, opened to the last page Roy had been reading. He could see the instructions on the preparation of the wood that was used to pierce Lukas' eye. It made sense to him. He realized there was more to the act than just blinding Lukas. The wood itself was damaging to him, would have dampened his ability to attack. *If it had stayed in long enough,* Steven thought.

He flipped through the book again. He found the section on protection, and yes, he could read some of it. He found the recipe for the potion Roy had given him. There were several items on the ingredients list he did not recognize, but none of them looked like rat shit. He was grateful.

As he continued to flip through the pages, some items jumped out at him. Many seemed to be related to creatures that transform. He read about a few of them. Some mimicked insects, and Steven wondered how many might be crawling or flying around in the world right now. Several were about small animals, the size of mice, that eventually formed a type of cocoon and slowly faded into invisibility, emerging as a ravenous bird that went about devouring other invisible creatures in the river. A couple of them were about entities that looked like humans, but evolved into something more evil, like Lukas. The idea that there were more Lukases out there, waiting to be dealt with, chilled him. *There are an awful lot of children that go missing every year,* he thought. *How horrible if any are consumed by these things.*

He shut the book, exhausted from just the short time he'd spent in it.

"Not for the weak hearted, is it?" Roy asked.

"No," Steven replied, "it isn't. There's some horrible stuff in here."

"And some good," Roy said. "You just haven't run into those parts yet. You will."

"Really?" Steven asked. "Is this something you think I should learn?"

"I don't know, you tell me. Should you?"

Steven thought this over. He didn't think this was a take-it-or-leave-it moment, but he knew Roy was hopeful he'd say yes. He didn't want to disappoint him, but at the same time he was unsure. There were a lot of questions.

"Tell me how you decided," he said to Roy.

"OK," Roy said. "Sure." He pulled up a chair next to Steven.

"I first saw this book when I was fourteen. I discovered it in my father's closet when I was trying to find his guns, which weren't in the closet because he kept them locked up in a cabinet, but I didn't know that. I stole it out of his room and took it to my own. I was fascinated by the workmanship of it, and its age. I couldn't make heads or tails of any of it, but there were a few drawings that caught my attention and I knew I was drawn to it. I forgot to put it back.

"He figured I had taken it, and he came into my room one night to confront me about it. He was as kind as could be, and when I confessed I'd found and taken it, he wasn't angry. He sat down next to me and asked me why I'd taken it, and I told him I thought it was impressive, and that I just wanted to browse through it. He asked me if I could read any of it, and I told him I couldn't. He asked me if I'd like to be able to read some of it, and I told him that yes, I would like to. A big smile spread across his face, and he told me he'd help me.

"My mother knew all about it. She didn't have the qualms that Claire had. She was supportive. I think she might have married my father because of it, to tell you the truth.

"That week my father showed me how to jump in. He didn't push me, it was my choice. He taught me what you could do in it, and how to maneuver. He had a few tricks that he showed me. I thought I had died and gone to heaven. None of my high school friends could do what I could do. But he taught me to keep it to myself, and I tried."

"Did you confront any entities together?" Steven asked. "Like we just did with Lukas?"

"Yes, several. The first was a ghost that inhabited a barn. A friend of Dad's had a barn that always spooked his horses. He had to fight with them to get them inside, and he asked my dad to take a look. Even though he always kept quiet about his gift, close friends always seemed to know. They could sense it. They wouldn't talk about it openly, but when there was a problem that needed solving, they would ask my dad. He always helped them."

"What happened with the ghost?" Steven asked, intrigued.

"Oh, the barn ghost. Well, sure enough, we saw what he meant. In the field these horses were passive and gentle. You could pet them, feed them, lead them around, no problem. But if you tried to take them into the barn, they'd rear up. They would not go in.

"My dad took me back to the barn one night, and sat a chair in the middle of it, kind of like I did with you in the hallway. He had me place a blindfold on his eyes, and gave me instructions not to interrupt him until he was done, but to make sure he didn't walk into something and hurt himself. He went into a trance and I watched him for an hour in that dark barn, and let me tell you, it was spooky. Good fun for a teenager, but still scary as hell. After a while I noticed the body, swinging from the rafters. It was the top half of a woman, hung by the neck. The bottom half was missing. Grisly sight. Gave me nightmares for weeks. But that was the information he needed to sort it out. Within a few days he'd solved the problem and the horses would go into the barn on their own."

Steven was enraptured with the story. "How did he solve it?"

"I don't know," Roy replied. "He never told me. At first he only involved me in the trance part. Later on, as we worked together more, he would let me see more of what he did. And he would show me parts of the book, as he recorded the things he'd done. And he'd explain other parts as I began to figure things out."

"Perhaps he figured," Steven said, "that a hanging woman was enough for the first experience of a fourteen-year-old."

"You're probably right," Roy replied. "It knocked my socks off. It was better than a whole year of horror movies at the cinema."

"Do you have friends that ask you to solve problems?" Steven asked Roy.

"Yes, I do. Not many, I couldn't do much and keep the promise I made to Claire. But I've helped a few friends since she died, and a few while she was alive, that I hid from her."

Steven paused. "Were you ever planning on showing this to me?" he asked.

Roy thought about this for a moment. "Yes," he said. "I always knew it would be you. I didn't know how or when it would happen, but I always thought at some point it would be you. You have the gift. I think you have it stronger than me."

Steven didn't argue, he just smiled. He had always known how to argue with Roy, and rarely agreed with him. This was one of those times when he didn't need to do either, but just let it stand.

◊

Steven sat on his deck, overlooking Lake Washington, sipping coffee. It was a rare sunny morning and the lake was unusually calm, the water flat and shiny. In the distance he could see an eagle flying over the trees in Seward Park. Things seemed peaceful, balanced.

In his own home, Steven had fixed the hallway floorboards and had put the rest of the house in order. Things seemed normal. He slept the last few nights without incident. He remembered opening his eyes while lying in bed, glancing at the places where the faces had appeared, wondering if they would come back. They didn't.

The downstairs bathroom was the most uncomfortable. The idea of Ben dying in that tub made him feel very sad. Steven didn't use it as much as the upstairs bathroom, so it was easy to avoid.

He still had Ben's journal. He had been reading more of it, especially the parts that followed his identification of Lukas as the culprit. The actual story of how Ben was able to subdue

Lukas and bury him wasn't in the journal, but Steven had found the part where he figured it had happened, because the tone changed dramatically, from anger to fear. He had constructed several ways in which Ben might have done it. Some involved heroics, others subterfuge, others brute force. None of them seemed right to him, but he felt compelled to fill in the blank spaces. He liked the heroic scenario, and let it sit in his brain. He knew it wasn't what really happened, but that didn't matter.

The sun was warming the air but it was still comfortably cool. He took another sip of coffee and glanced out over the water. No one was on the lake, and it looked like a giant mirror, reflecting the green of the trees that surrounded it.

Steven knew he would spend more time with his father from now on. What they had gone though was the ultimate father-son bonding experience. He had learned how resilient his old man was, and how he had misjudged him for so long. There was so much he still didn't know about him, and he resolved to find out.

Then there was the book, and Roy's knowledge. Steven knew Roy intended to train him, to give him the knowledge he possessed. Steven welcomed it. He wasn't sure where his career or his love life might lead him, but he knew this was a new, unexpected dimension of his life, and he was ready to absorb whatever Roy felt like passing along. It was exciting to him, more exciting than anything that had happened to him since his divorce.

Maybe since before that, he thought. *Maybe more exciting than anything else in my life.*

Looking over the small ripples that now began to form on the lake, Steven imagined the flow, and pictured it in his mind. He fell into it, and floated, waiting to see what would occur. He heard the sound of birds, amplified. When he was on the bank he could hear them, but couldn't see them – now in the river, he knew exactly where they were, what type of bird they were. He could move to where they were perched without disturbing them. He could fly with them, if he chose.

He heard the sounds of his neighbors. The sentences and comments of everyday domesticity emerged and he suddenly felt like a spy. He was surprised at how easy it was to fine tune his hearing. He knew he could move inside their houses if he wanted, but he didn't want to violate their privacy. And he knew that there were more ghosts in houses nearby, and he was through with ghosts for a while.

He turned his attention back to the lake, and imagined what it would be like to be buried under water. In a rush he was transported into the lake, and he instinctively held his breath. Water enveloped him, cold and dark. Large green plants brushed against his feet, and he could see a salmon swim above him. He sunk into the cold earth below the lake, and felt the darkness surround him. *This is hell,* he thought.

He emerged from the flow, and felt his headache return. He drank more coffee. The pain was substantially less than the first few times he'd jumped in, and it dissipated more rapidly. He had the sensation of having just completed a morning workout.

Michael still worried him. It was like when you leave for a trip, and have a nagging feeling you've left something at home that you should have brought. But he had learned to trust Roy. Roy was far more experienced with people like Michael. Trusting Roy had been hard to do at first, but now Steven found it easier. The old man was a cranky sonofabitch, but he loved him and knew he should heed his advice.

He stood on the bank once more, ready to dive back into the flow. The bank was losing its attraction to him, and the river was becoming a place of immense pleasure and discovery. His skepticism now seemed like a crutch, a way to justify denying himself these new experiences. Jumping in felt like freedom from constraints he had placed upon himself.

He glanced back over the lake, its calmness reassuring him. He watched the people moving around the path that circled the lake, some jogging, some pushing strollers, some just walking, solo. He felt sorry for them all. He felt liberated. He felt like a new man.

Michael Richan lives in Seattle, Washington.

◊

Steven and Roy work together to confront the ghosts of
Mason Manor in the next book of *The River* series,

A Haunting in Oregon.

◊

Visit

www.michaelrichan.com

◊

Did you enjoy this book?
The author would love to know your opinion of the book.
Please leave your review at Amazon.com and Goodreads.com.
Your feedback is appreciated!

Made in the USA
Charleston, SC
25 September 2013